Ten-in-One

A CIRCUS SALMAGUNDI ANTHOLOGY

KIM BANNERMAN

Copyright © 2024 by Kim Bannerman

ISBN (print): 978-1-998567-00-3

ISBN (ebook): 978-1-998567-01-0

All rights reserved. No part of this book may be reproduced or transmitted in any form or by any means, electronically or mechanical, including photocopying, recording, or by any information storage and retrieval system, without permission in writing from the copyright owner.

This is a work of fiction. All names, characters, places and incidents either are the product of the author's imagination or are used fictitiously, and any resemblance to any actual person, living or dead, is entirely coincidental.

This book was created in Canada.

For more information, contact kim@kbannerman.com.

Books by Kim Bannerman

The Lizzie Saunders series

Bucket of Blood
Mark of the Magpie
The Agony of St. Alice

The Circus Salmagundi Series

Truly the Devil's Work
The Vengeful Dead
The Sea Will Have
Knife and Bone
Ten-In-One
Under a Copper Sun

Other titles

The Tattooed Wolf
The Fire Song
Love and Lovecraft
The Blackwood Papers
Aeterna
small seasons

Contents

Prologue	1
1. Of Sheep and Sasquatch	3
2. Blurpy	12
3. Nothing More to Give	19
4. Farewell: A Lion's Tale	35
5. Snakes and Ladders	47
6. What Walks at Barrow Lake	54
7. Forever Underground	71
8. The Cat and the Karluk	84
9. The Business of Flesh and Blood	102
10. The Merrow	123
11. The Fate of the Alpha	132
Acknowledgments	137

To Ellie, Jonathan and Desmond, who listened and asked excellent questions, and helped pull these stories together.

Prologue

Aw, crap, I accidentally wrote another book.

Let me explain.

While walking on an autumn night in 2019, a bolt of inspiration hit me right between the eyes, and in that singular moment, the Circus Salmagundi mystery series began. The concept appeared fully formed and spoiling for a fight, much like Athena springing from Zeus' noggin. Fairly quickly, I was scribbling ideas on slips of paper, pulling together characters and exploring their relationships, and crafting histories for each of the major players. Some of these notes swiftly expanded into short stories. They were drafted in a flurry of excitement and optimism, without boundaries or restrictions, and never meant for public consumption.

I wrote the first three novels in rapid succession and released them all in 2021. The fourth novel in the series appeared in 2023.

In 2024, when Jamie Bryant and Elian Bell at CVOX Radio asked me if I'd like to read a story over the air, I was intrigued. I'd already dabbled in podcasting, and I'd been toying with the idea of creating an audio book. Making a radio show would give me a good excuse to start recording, but reading out a full novel seemed like a big jump. Plus, I was in the middle of some large projects that already demanded sizeable chunks of my weekly schedule, and I was halfway through writing the fifth Circus Salmagundi novel, *Under a Copper Sun*. There's only so many hours in a day! I decided that a novel might be too much... but what about short stories?

The aforementioned bundle of short stories sat half-forgotten in my desk, and I wondered if they might prove useful. Why not dust them off and polish them up?

I took a few of the stories and edited them, sent them to friends and family members for feedback, then recorded them in our home studio. Shawn Pigott produced them and added musical interludes. We sent these to Marc Gerrard at CVOX, to be released over the airwaves each week as the radio program 'Story and Song'. It was a lot of fun!

But when it was done, I really didn't want it to end. I love these stories! They aren't mysteries or murders, but they still celebrate the weirder elements of British Columbia's history, and fold together strong personalities with strange situations and beautiful, mist-shrouded landscapes. I convinced myself that six short stories might work well together as a print anthology. If the main mystery novels are the Big Top extravaganza, then this anthology is the sideshow.

Ah ha! Eureka! The sideshow in the Circus Salmagundi is called the 'Ten-in-One', a collection of ten sequential acts in a single tent, and that might make a perfectly lovely title for a book... why not write another four stories to round out the anthology, just for good measure? And as a bonus, maybe throw in an extra story from long ago? I wrote *The Fate of the Alpha* when I was working on *Bucket of Blood*, and it seemed to play well with the rest of these tales.

Thus, 'Ten-In-One' was born. I didn't mean to write an anthology; it just kinda happened.

That's my story and I'm sticking to it.

Of Sheep and Sasquatch

"Mr. Grady?"

A circle of faces looked up at the old roustabout, each one warm and amber-tinged by the light of the crackling bonfire. He searched among them for the source of the wee voice.

"What is it, Mary?" he said.

She was small for 9-years-old. She wore a winter pinafore and apron, still dusty from playing baseball in the shorn hayfield. Her older brother Hugo sat to her left, and her older sister Martha sat to her right. The air smelled of impending snow and the ocean was the colour of a whetstone, but the land remained dry, and when the Circus Salmagundi spent its off-season at the farm in Cedar-By-The-Sea, the children showed their appreciation for any sunny day – no matter how cold -- by playing outside for hours.

The adults were much the same. With the boats tied up at the dock, the dancing horses put out to pasture, and the wide starry sky still clear of clouds, what a great and simple pleasure it was to enjoy an evening bonfire on the beach! There might be fiddle music; there was certainly ale and roasted apples sprinkled with cinnamon. Lou glanced across his audience. He noted Stella the Bearded Lady, and Nancy the pony-trainer, and Bill Peacock the knife thrower. Two stagehands, Robert

Mackenzie and Toot Simmons, were already deep in their cups and very jolly. Even Mary's father, Grover Scott, circus owner and boss of this whole darn outfit, had joined them at the fire tonight! Everyone was mellow and in good spirits. Folks had recently finished dinner and, satisfied with full bellies, they wanted a story to entertain them before they turned in for the night.

Lou Grady, a natural raconteur, was always willing to oblige.

But Mary had a habit of speaking softly and stumbling over her words. She was so timid!

"Last night you told us a story 'bout the sasquatch," she said, the complicated sounds tripping over her tongue. "But then I didn't sleep so good. I had nightmares that it was peeking in the portholes of the boat! Is tonight's story gonna be frightful, too?"

A few of the adults around the bonfire muttered their agreement. Yes, a mild tale would be better.

Lou scowled, not at the girl, but at the audience. None of them would complain or admit to being spooked, but they were happy enough to let the timid little girl ask. Why not save face and let her seem weak?

'Bloody cowards!' he thought.

He crouched down to speak to Mary, eye to eye. "How about this, my luv," he began gently, "I'll tell you a true tale."

"But you said the sasquatch tale was true," she replied. "That's what kept me awake!"

A crooked grin deepened the wrinkles around his mouth. "Then I'll tell you a true tale, but without any monsters. A tale about a boat, much like our own *SS Nona*." He gestured along the slope of the beach to the dock where the *Nona* was tethered. "Would that be better?"

"Oh, yes, please," she said with relief. She had a cherub's face, and when she smiled, her eyes sparkled. Other adults and children nodded. A pleasant tale about a steamship would be much appreciated.

Lou scanned their self-satisfied faces as they settled back on logs and deck chairs, snuggled into their blankets with mugs of hot tea or cocoa in hand, eager for a soothing story.

Bloody cowards, he thought once more. Then, giving a smirk too sly to be friendly, he began...

TEN-IN-ONE

I'm gonna tell ya the story of the steamboat *Clallam*, which much like our *SS Nona*, was part of the Mosquito Fleet that putters around the Puget Sound. These fine ferries link all the towns and ports from Seattle to Victoria, and you'll recognize them by their fancy white paint with crisp black trim. It's a fine and proud fleet, 'though some of the boats are a little slow at times. You've no doubt heard the poem about that somewhat ponderous side-wheeler, the *George E. Starr*, which we see off our bow on occasion:

> Paddle, paddle, George E. Starr,
> How we wonder where you are.
> Leaves Seattle at half past ten.
> Gets to Bellingham, God knows when!
> As you creep across the bight,
> We can see your masthead light,
> Out upon the bay so far,
> Paddle, paddle George E. Starr.

Now, the *George E. Starr* is an older boat, built in the 1870s, but the *SS Clallam* took to the water in April 1903 – only a few years before our lad Hugo here was born! The ship was crafted from good, solid Douglas fir at a shipyard in Tacoma, and at 168-feet long, she was outfitted with an 800-horsepower compound engine that gave her a cruising speed of 13 knots. A solid and serviceable vessel, then, and perfect for our calm inland waters.

She wasn't extravagant, but she was clean and tidy, with a single smoke stack and that same fancy black-and-white paint job. She was licensed to carry 250 passengers and freight, but without freight, the number could be pushed to 500. She had 44 elegant staterooms, 6 large lifeboats and 530 life preservers, 25 fire buckets, 4 life buoys, 6 axes, and 6 emergency lanterns. Now, that's a lot of numbers to remember, but all you need to know is this: *Clallam* ran a no-nonsense, straight-forward, simple and circular route from Tacoma to Seattle, to Port Townsend and Victoria, then back again. Such a short and simple circuit around the Puget Sound offered few challenges for an accomplished crew.

But right from the beginning, things started to go wrong.

When the *Clallam* was launched, the flag of the United States was hauled up the main mast for the very first time, but as it unfurled, everyone in the crowd saw that it had been hung upside-down. Oh, I hear the gasp from you sea-faring men – an upside-down flag is a distress signal! Hardly a good omen for the ship! Then, 14-year-old Hazel Beahan was asked to break a bottle of champagne across the bow to christen the ship, which we all know bestows good fortune on the vessel... but oh no! When the blocks were knocked away, the *Clallam* slid into the ocean too quickly, and Hazel swung the bottle but missed the boat.

Mariners are a superstitious bunch at the best of times. Both the flag and the champagne were clear signs of wicked luck to come.

For seven months, the *Clallam* ran her route without incident, through the summer and into the fall. Weather was clement, conditions were good, no one had any inkling that a disaster was on its way.

So came the morning of Friday, January 8th, 1904, a fine enough day for winter on the west coast: a little cold, a little wet, but nothing a good yellow slicker won't repel. At Seattle's Pier 1, at the foot of Yesler Way, the *Clallam* began loading northbound passengers and freight. Nothing was out of the ordinary, nothing was amiss, until the first hint of impending doom made itself known in a most cheerful and whimsical way.

As you know, the Mosquito Fleet carries livestock from port to port, and on this particular voyage, a flock of sheep was to be delivered to Port Townsend before the ship carried on to Victoria. Sheep can be skittish and difficult to load so, to encourage the dumb animals to board, sailors use a trained ewe wearing a bell to guide the flock. The bell-sheep knows that boarding a ship isn't a scary thing to do. With its collar and a copper bell around its wooly neck, it encourages the other ewes to load in an orderly fashion.

On this morning, though, Billy the bell-sheep refused to board.

Nothing the crew did could persuade that blessed creature to budge. They pushed, they prodded, they tried to coax Billy with sugar cubes and liquor. Nothing! The bell-sheep braced its hooves and refused to set a single teeny-tiny hoof on the *Clallam*'s gangplank.

Schedules are tight. They had places to be. They couldn't wait a minute longer.

When the *Clallam* departed Seattle at precisely 8:30 am, the sheep were left behind.

Other than this little hiccup, everything seemed to be going jim-dandy. Captain George Roberts was an experienced gent with a balding crown and bushy black beard. He'd sailed for over 29 years, and he knew these waters like the back of his salt-weathered hand. The *Clallam* picked up passengers and freight at Port Townsend, cleared customs, then just after noon, turned her bow north across the Strait of Juan de Fuca, bound for Victoria. Captain Roberts was quite certain, the *Clallam* would reach Victoria by 4:00 p.m.

But the wind was starting to rise, my luvs, and the snow was starting to fall, and the Strait of Juan de Fuca can be a nasty place in the midst of a January storm.

Mary peered at him askance like a curious crow.

"Did they really give liquor and sugar cubes to a sheep?" she asked, crossing her arm.

Lou stuttered to a stop.

"You don't believe me?"

She scowled but didn't answer. A few adults prompted him to continue. Lou clapped his hands and righted himself, remembering where he was in his story. As he began again, he made a mental note to check his facts next time he was in Seattle. Did they ply Billy the sheep with liquor and sugar cubes? Or had he made that up, and simply convinced himself over the years that it was true?

Lou couldn't recall – but he weren't no teacher, nor scientist, nor historian! He was a storyteller, by God, and a good storyteller never lets a little truth get in the way of a good yarn.

Now, Tatoosh Island is actually a group of rocky islets – little more than a few spires of bare stone – that sit half a mile offshore from Cape Flattery, right at the entrance where the wild Pacific Ocean funnels into Juan de Fuca Strait. The only building on Tatoosh is a lighthouse, called the Cape Flattery Light, which was built in 1857. Oh, it's a lonely place, indeed! As it's the north-westernmost lighthouse on the West Coast of the contiguous United States, the place sits out in the choppy green waters with nothing around it but cantankerous gulls and pea-soup fog and the howl of that miserable wind.

The very same morning that the sailors were fighting with the sheep to board the ship, the Cape Flattery Light measured the wind speed at 60 miles an hour. A freezing mix of snow and rain started to fall. These were miserable conditions to be at sea, and as the *Clallam* entered the Strait, it met gale force winds and heavy swells, crashing across the bow. Still, it plugged steadily on, slowly but surely, across 35 miles of open water.

I suppose the captain felt they had a job to do, and he wasn't about to let a little ocean spray and a gusty breeze turn him back. But as the weather worsened, perhaps he gave a thought to the nervous bell-sheep, and wondered if such a stupid creature was, perhaps, not so stupid after all!

By 2 pm, a porthole broke on the starboard side. The *Clallam* began taking on water. The bilge pumps were fired up and the broken window was stuffed with blankets, but it did no good: salt-chuck flowed into the engine room, and by the time Captain Roberts arrived to assess the damage, he was waist deep in freezing water. Coal bunkers were awash. Pumps were clogged with debris. God almighty, what a sight!

By 3 pm, water reached the boilers and extinguished the fires, killing the engines. Even though they were within sight of Victoria's Clover Point, the accursed *Clallam* wallowed in the high swells, unable to move.

Waves pounding on the sideboards. The glass of the portholes creaked and cried. The crew feared the ship would break apart at the seams. Captain

Roberts made a desperate decision: load the women and children into lifeboats and send them off the collapsing ship to the safety of the shore. By golly, there was no time to waste! Passengers loaded into three lifeboats and the stalwart crew began lowering them on the lee side. Surely, this was the best course of action. After all, they were only a couple of miles from land!

But as the first boat lowered, it struck a guardrail on the ship. The lifeboat tipped over. The occupants spilled into the sea. The women wore heavy dresses and wool coats, and unable to swim in the fearsome waves, they were all dragged under and claimed by Neptune. The second boat managed to get away, but as they headed for Discovery Island, a gigantic wave swamped the lifeboat and it sank, too. Finally, the third lifeboat was cast off, but it became entangled in ropes. As the men aboard the *Clallam* watched helplessly, it capsized, as well. None of the lifeboat passengers survived.

Lou took a moment to moisten his lips with a sip of ale. He knew a story's power was often enhanced by the teller's sense of timing, so he paused to savour the tension in the air. A dreadful silence had fallen around the campfire.

Grover Scott broke the stillness. "Come on, man," he said, "Is this the right tale to tell? We all live on ships!"

"Just as I promised, sir, this story has no monsters," said Lou.

"Maybe not," said Grover, "But holy hell!"

"Now, now," Lou tutted, "There's nothing wrong with a true story, if it can teach the children something important."

"And what important lesson can this possibly share?" said Grover in exasperation.

Lou set down his glass. "The lesson? Well, that's easy, sir," he replied. "Pay heed to nervous sheep! Now, where was I..."

Ah, yes! Onshore, around 5 pm, a couple of folks spotted the *Clallam* floundering near Trial Island, pushed eastward by the wind. Rolling and listing in the waves, she was obviously dead in the water.

The Puget Sound Navigation Company had an agent in Victoria, a fella by the name of Edward Blackwood, and he sent out a desperate plea for help. He tried to rustle up tugboats and steamers to lend aid, but none were available or ready to sail. Darkness was falling, the storm was growing stronger. Finally, he located one ship that was able to attempt a rescue: the *SS Iroquois* out of Sidney, BC. The *Iroquois* set out immediately, but in the dark storm, it was almost impossible to see anything, and to make matters worse, the *Clallam* carried no rockets to show her location. Despite many gruelling hours weaving through the San Juan islands, the crew of the *Iroquois* couldn't spot the *Clallam*. Defeated, empty-handed, and severely damaged by the storm, the *Iroquois* was forced to limp home.

But while the *Iroquois* had failed to locate the *Clallam*, two other tugboats had spotted her and were attempting a rescue in the dark of night: the *Richard Holyoke* from Port Townsend and the *Sea Lion* from Seattle. With difficulty, the *Richard Holyoke* approached the struggling *Clallam* and threw her a towline, intending to drag her back to Port Townsend. Captain Roberts agreed to the plan but forgot to mention that the *Clallam* was sinking. As they moved forward in the ocean, she continued to rapidly take on water, and when the tow line slackened, she veered abruptly, tipped over on her side, and quickly started to capsize.

By God, the *Clallam* was going to take the *Richard Holyoke* down with her! In a rush, sailors climbed onto the sides to hack away at the ropes with axes. Waves crashed over the boat and swept the men away. The *Clallam* broke into pieces as the remaining passengers leapt into the hungry sea.

Now, there was no time to lose! A stout and hearty man in the freezing waters of wintertime lasts only a few minutes before he succumbs to the cold. The two tugboats rushed to pluck survivors from the waves, but for all their valour, they were only able to rescue 14 passengers and 22 crewmen. In the days following the disaster, the island, shorelines, and waters were searched exhaustively for survivors, but search parties recovered the bodies of only 28 victims. The rest were never found.

And that was not the end of the *Clallam*'s bad luck, my luvs. Remember how I said the *Iroquois* sustained damage from trying to help? Well, only a few years later, the *Iroquois* sank under similar conditions during a storm in the Gulf Islands, with 14 people drowned. Now, whether that was due to the damage she'd sustained, or just that she'd taken on a bit of the *Clallam*'s bad fortune, who can say?

The circle of faces around the bonfire were still cast in a comforting glow, but rather than anticipation or relaxation, each member of the audience looked tense and horrified. A few of the younger children wept silently, clinging to their mothers for comfort. Grover Scott glared at Lou in a most threatening manner. Lou wondered if his pay might be docked a few dollars. He didn't mind. It was a small cost to pay for a good story.

Mary sat snugly between her brother and sister. Her arms were crossed. Any trace of a smile had vanished completely.

Lou took a sip of beer. "Well, Mary, my luv?" he said, raising one brow. "Whadya think of that tale?"

She glared at him with dark, ferocious, rueful eyes: a particularly determined expression he'd never seen on her cherub's face before.

"If that's your idea of a better story, Mr. Grady," she said, "I prefer the sasquatch."

Plurpy

Seeing poor Martin diminish from a brawny teenage boy to a scrawny sack of bones nearly broke his mother's heart.

Like his three older brothers, Martin was a stout and stalwart child with a healthy appetite and a wanton lust for dangerous pastimes. He loved to climb the cliffs near their house on the big island – the place had once been called 'Chuan Island', but then changed to 'Admiral Island' to commemorate some stuffy British naval commander. When they were young, the boys would pretend to be naval officers, but this soon changed to pirates, which allowed for more thievery and rough-housing. As they grew older, the boys practiced jumping from the back of one cantering horse to another in the pasture. Martin allowed his brothers to shoot at him with pellet guns while he sprinted through the raspberry canes, dodging their assault and emitting yelps when their aim was true. The Spindle Boys were gregarious children that encouraged each other to take the most outrageous risks: the more outrageous, the more boisterous was their laughter. Folks across the island argued whether they were brave or stupid, but any mother would be proud to have such a brood of energetic sons.

Of course, as well as proud, Mrs. Spindle was also very tired.

To keep the boys from under foot, she encouraged them to play outdoors. It was the only way to exhaust them. She also ordered them to help their father in the barbershop, but Mr. Spindle was not a patient man, and he'd soon chase them away after annoying his clients. And she baked pies – dozens upon dozens of pies – to keep them fed and full. Meat, fruit, fish: whatever she could stick between two crusts. Mrs. Spindle baked a lot of pies, and with this constant practice, she became famous across the Gulf Islands for her delicious culinary creations.

Martin's favourite was a blueberry-rhubarb-peach combination, sprinkled with brown sugar and cinnamon. As a toddler, he called it a 'blue-rhoo-pea-pie', and then shortened this further to 'blurpy'. Martin could polish off an entire blurpy in one sitting without sharing a single slice, and feel no guilt at all.

What the boys didn't eat, she sold. Thank goodness their father pulled in a decent wage! There weren't many pies to sell once the boys got into them, and Martin ate more than his fair share.

But all that changed when he was thirteen years old.

In the summer of 1910, a pharmacist came to the island to hawk his wares. His name was Dr. Franz Krause, and he had recently arrived from Germany, and brought with him a shipment of a miracle tonic which his noble and illustrious family had developed and sold back in the Old Country – "Doctor Krause's Liquid Lightning", he called it. He proclaimed that one bottle of watery ichor would revive, rejuvenate, and resuscitate anyone suffering from a host of maladies: gout, gripe, congestion, consumption, constipation, cankers, carbuncles and cancer. If you couldn't sleep, it would lull you to dreamland. If you slept too much, it put a zip in your step. And in the bedroom...well! Ladies never complained! Doctor Krause's Liquid Lightning enlivened the marriage vows and left a satisfied grin on everyone's face.

Dr. Krause found a curious but cautious audience on Admiral Island. He sold a score of his tiny brown bottles: not as much product as he'd hoped, but as he was packing up his wares to continue on his journey when he noticed the Spindle boys climbing the outside of the church steeple. Maybe, thought Krause, the island had more to offer him than just crass riches.

The pharmacist introduced himself to the lads, hanging off the side of the church. They chatted briefly, and Krause was much impressed by

Mrs. Spindle's boys – polite and clever, if a little rambunctious. He offered to take one with him on tour down the West Coast, to help him hawk his wares and educate the world about the miraculous, multifaceted benefits of Liquid Lightning. Waggling his artfully-plucked eyebrows, he promised to pay his new assistant handsomely.

Money? And one less mouth to feed? Mrs. Spindle would be an idiot to say no! But she needed the two oldest boys to help on the farm, and the second-youngest was already learning his father's trade. That left Martin. Mrs. Spindle thought, yes, Martin made the best choice. After all, Martin ate the most out of all of them.

The next day, Martin Spindle bid his family farewell and joined Dr. Krause on the pharmaceutical circuit.

Between them, they cooked up a fine story: in their fiction, Martin had been an ill boy, all noodle-armed and flabby-stomached, before embarking on a daily regime of Liquid Lightning. A single dose, every morning before breakfast, and KER-POW! Dr. Krause's delicious, delectable mineral infusion returned him to fine health within a week. The specimen of boyish exuberance capering around centre-stage was the result! When Krause came to the end of this monologue, Martin dashed back a bottle of Liquid Lightning, then polished off a couple of steak-and-kidney pies to show the strength of his appetite and, letting out a moist belch to the laughter of the audience, he executed a series of flips and summersaults. Finally, the boy would bow graciously to waves of applause, and Krause would pull out the money box. The results were always the same. The cheering audience would push forward with dollars in hand. Krause and Martin would leave town, much richer than when they entered it.

Martin loved the attention. He loved to move his body in strange and wonderful ways. He certainly loved steak-and-kidney pie! And he didn't even mind the taste of Doctor Krause's Liquid Lightning – it was a little tart, but not too sour. Every night, he watched Krause whip up a new batch of the concoction, so he knew the ingredients were harmless: Krause took an old earthenware pot from his suitcase and filled it with water from the pump of that evening's boarding house. Then, he'd drop a tiny lump of silver-white metal into the pot and let it sit for an hour. The metal, Krause claimed, had fallen from heaven many years ago. His forefathers passed down the meteorite and the earthenware pot from generation to generation, performing this same arcane ritual to leech its cosmic powers into a potent elixir that imparted long, radiant lives. Why, he'd heard his great-grandfather had lived to the age of 153!

"No!" said Martin as they bottled the concoction.

"It's true!" Krause replied.

When they finished bottling the ichor, Krause carefully wrapped the meteorite in a length of cotton, painted with lead. Then he tucked the tiny bundle safely in his suitcase, and held his finger to his lips.

"Now, this secret to long life is yours, too!"

"Will I live to be 153?" the boy asked in a reverential hush, counting on his fingers. "That's... that's... that's the year of our Lord, two-thousand and fifty!"

"Imagine the wonders you'll see!" Krause replied with a twinkle in his eye.

This same daily ritual was repeated for three whole months. Every afternoon, they gave the same performance in a new town and, every night, they bottled more of the wondrous brew while dreaming up fantastical visions of the distant future.

As they travelled down the West Coast, through Washington and Oregon, Dr. Krause could hardly suppress his delight. His suitcase jangled with coins and crumpled dollars. It's easy to be a generous man when your pockets are full, and Krause paid Martin twice the agreed rate, which the boy promptly sent home to his mother. The boy had little need for money. For Martin, the better treasure was all the positive effects of Liquid Lightning as it coursed through his bloodstream: a smooth complexion, a spring to his step, a radiant glow to his sparkling eyes. He felt himself growing stronger. He knew he was going to live forever, striding forward with confidence into a world of wonders!

They made it as far as Monterey before Martin began to falter.

Dr. Krause noticed first: Martin's trousers seemed to hang off his hips, and what had once been a pair of firm calves now appeared a little wasted. Martin waved away the pharmacist's concern. His feet had been giving him some troubles – his toes were numb in the morning -- but it was nothing that a strong massage couldn't fix.

But the calves...

Krause was perplexed by this reaction to his family's famed mineral waters.

Over the next week, Martin's health declined. Nothing dreadful or dramatic like smallpox or syphilis, of course, but a noticeable thinning of his limbs, an unsteady wobble to his step, a garish knobbiness to his knees. Krause suggested they take a few days rest at an elderly friend's mansion near Salinas.

Martin didn't want that at all! He craved the cheers of the audience. He loved the sound of the girls, swooning in the front row. What boy in his right mind would choose to trade the adoration of pretty young ladies for a quiet sanitarium populated by a bunch of old people?

But that first night in Salinas, he started to sweat and shake. His appetite remained as voracious as ever, but now, nothing seemed to satisfy him. Krause ordered beef tongue and roasted onions, duck in orange sauce and green grapes fresh off the vine, but none of the food quelled poor Martin's ravenous hunger. Another bottle of Liquid Lightning failed to restore him.

After three days, Krause was quite concerned. Martin no longer possessed the strength to crawl out of bed. Hunger made him crazy. His bugged eyes were wild and desperate. A grey pallor crossed his face. In a fit of guilt, Krause admitted to Martin that he was no pharmacist, and that his credentials were as much a fiction as their marketing ploy – his name wasn't even Franz Krause, it was Bob Murgatroyd, and the special lump from which his potions got their powers had not been passed down over the centuries through his esteemed noble family, but purchased for twenty bucks in the alley behind a medical lab in Cleveland.

Frankly, Martin was too weak to be angry. His ribs looked like canvas stretched over a tent frame. His cheekbones stuck out like gull wings. He could barely lift his skinny hands. And most alarming of all, when the room was very dark, he was sure he was starting to glow.

By day four, terror seized Krause when he realized, the boy was going to die in his care. All his hard-earned money would be lost. The authorities might even confiscate the mineral lump from which he distilled his miracle cure.

He wrapped the boy up in a blanket and took him by carriage to the docks at Monterey. Before pressing a wad of bills into the boy's frail hand and booting him out of the carriage, Martin heard Krause say, "You must understand, I can't go back to prison! Not again!"

Martin was too weak to stand, but he had money to spend and a clear destination in mind. A couple of kindly fishermen agreed to take the boy as far north as San Francisco, where he'd find a steamer bound for Victoria, BC.

Those next few days vanished in a hazy blur. Martin felt half-starved, desperate to fill his belly and stave off the stomach cramps. He lay curled in a bunk below decks, raving and snarling and cursing Krause's name to the winds. The fishermen were religious men, and they crossed themselves whenever they came close to Martin, because in the low illumination below-decks he gave off a particular greenish cast. The captain claimed to have seen such a glow before: it was St. Elmo's Fire, like when the mast of a ship glows during the height of a storm -- a token of divine providence and a promise of good fortune to come.

By the time Martin boarded the steam ship in San Francisco, most of his muscles had withered away. His hair had fallen out in patches. He was able to pluck two teeth from his gums. He wanted nothing but to die, and he would've jumped into the sea, if he'd been strong enough to crawl over the ship railings.

The crew dumped him in Victoria, where he managed to beg passage to Admiral Island, only to discover it had been renamed 'Salt Spring Island' while he was gone. A man who regularly visited the barber shop recognized Martin's gaunt face, and rolled him into a wheelbarrow before pushing him home to his mother. By then, the insane hunger filled every crack and crevasse of the boy's mortal coil. Martin could barely form a single cohesive thought, except for one: blurpy.

He muttered this word when his mother lifted his bird-boned body and carried him to bed, emitting teary prayers while peppering his brow with loving kisses. He muttered this word when his three brothers came to stare at him, gap-mouthed and speechless, terrified by this skeletal version of their beloved youngest sibling. And he muttered this word when his father vowed to hunt down that damnable conman and plunge his barber scissors into the charlatan's neck.

His mother knew precisely what to do. She made him blurpy -- and blurpy, he ate in abundance!

As much as she could bake, he devoured. Housewives and gardeners from across the Gulf Islands brought gifts of blueberries and rhubarb to her door. A hundred glass jars of canned peaches appeared – enough for a hundred pies. She kneaded pastry dough, rolled out long circles, cut and pinched and sprinkled sugar and nutmeg. The oven didn't cool for days.

Every pie she carefully crafted disappeared down Martin's gullet. Every slice restored a little fraction of his strength. The islanders whispered that her pies were mystical things, full of delicious magic, and able to resurrect the dead.

Of course this wasn't true, and Mrs. Spindle would never be so audacious as to repeat the claim, but she took great secret joy in hearing it. Her pies were delicious, but they couldn't replace the flesh from Martin's bones, nor did it restore the vitality that he'd lost. There would never again be summersaults and flips, vaulting from horse to horse, or climbing up the outside of the church steeple. Doctor Krause's Liquid Lightning had stolen that from him.

But Mother Spindle's blurpy had yanked Martin back from death's doorstep, and restored in him a zest for living, and a yearning to perform -- and an irrepressible craving for pie. His tongue turned purple. His smile returned. The eerie, ghostly glow that had emanated from his clammy skin eventually faded, to be replaced by a pair of rosy cheeks. Martin Spindle would spend the rest of his days as a mere fraction of his former physical self, but while it might not last 153 years, his was a life that still held the promise of joy and beauty and pie, and for that, he was truly blessed.

Nothing More to Give

In August 1910, an envelope addressed to Argos Theos arrived by post. He read the return address with growing excitement and mistook this as a card for his 19th birthday, which fell at the end of the month. After all, his Uncle Ozias was the most exciting human being to ever travel the world, and a letter from him was sure to be a thrilling, if infrequent, delight.

But it wasn't a card. It wasn't even a letter.

The young man carefully unfolded the sheaf of papers, hearing the dry old fibres crackle as they resisted.

"What has that laze-about Ozias sent you now?" said his manoula in Greek. Her frustration bubbled much like the iron pot of beef stiffado, big enough to last the week, which she stirred erratically with a long wooden spoon. The kitchen was so cramped, he feared she might accidentally hit him with it, even though he sat at the table.

Argos replied in English. "I don't know. It looks very old."

The paper was roughly square, about the size of his hand, and covered in little marks and dashes, as well as two distinct, squiggling lines. It carried a few words written in pencil, but not in a language that he recognized.

She cursed and complained, still in florid Greek, and Argos only caught a few words here and there. They'd emigrated to Vancouver – him, his mother, and his uncle -- when he was only nine years old, and his grasp of his first language was solid but unsophisticated. However, he understood enough to know that she wanted nothing to do with her wayward brother. Maybe her curiosity burned deeply inside her, but her good sense demanded she remain vigilant.

"Is it a letter?"

"No," Argos replied in wonder. "Just this bit of paper. What do you think it means?"

She scoffed. "Don't you let him beguile you," she warned Argos in Greek. "He's half-crazy, that one!"

"Touched by the Gods," Argos replied in English.

His manoula didn't speak a word of English. She ignored Argos when he spoke that choppy, undignified, barbaric tongue. With a huff, she returned to seasoning her stew.

"If it's not a letter, then throw it out," she said, returning all her attention to her cooking. "He does not need to be sending all his junk to us!"

But the young man was intrigued.

Argos withdrew to their tiny front porch and sat on the top step of their walk-up apartment, which gave a fine (if cluttered) view over the rooftops of a delicatessen and a fish market. Suffocating in the stuffy August heat, he pondered the marks on the crusty paper. Was it a map? Of what, he couldn't tell. He recognized one squiggly line as a river, a childish drawing of a fish to show water, and perhaps the wrinkled form of a coastline. The faint words were in Spanish. He was fluent in English, and fairly good at Greek, and he could muddle his way through Egyptian and Turkish, but Spanish? No, he couldn't read it. He turned it around in his hands -- up down every which way -- trying to decipher its meaning, but all efforts were fruitless. Why his crazy uncle sent him an old map was a complete mystery to Argos.

Luckily, two days later, a bedraggled Ozias appeared on their doorstep to explain.

Argos' manoula was furious.

"What do you think you're doing?" she said to her brother in rapid Greek, then followed it with curses that Argos couldn't follow.

Ozias only laughed. He sat at the table and ate bowl after bowl of beef stiffado. He'd lost a great deal of weight since he'd left to go traveling, many months ago, and his face was thin and bony.

"You cannot take my little Argos from me," she continued, "He is my baby! He must stay and help take care of me!"

"First of all," said Ozias, "He's not little. What are you now, boy – 7 feet tall? A giant!" Ozias gulped down another mouthful. "Secondly, he is not a baby, but a man, and can make up his own mind. Thirdly," and here, the man openly scoffed, "You don't need anyone's help, Iola. You never have."

Her face screwed up with disgust. She tapped out her answers on her fingers.

"He is not 7 feet tall; he is 6 foot 8," she snapped. "He is not yet 19-years-old, and that makes him *almost* a man. And yes, I don't need anyone's help, but I love my boy and I don't want him hurt." Argos sat across from his uncle at the kitchen table, and his mother planted a smooch on the top of his head and laid her wrinkled hands on his burly shoulders. "I did not bring him all the way here from Greece to the safety of this country, so that you could throw him into danger."

"I'm not taking him out of the country, Iola," said Ozias. "The map, boy. Where is it?"

Argos had left the paper on the floor next to his bed. He fetched it.

"Good, good," said Ozias, unfolding it roughly, "This coastline, do you recognize it?"

But Argos shook his head. So did Iola.

Ozias glanced to his sister. "I visited the Sanctuary of Atotonilco, near San Miguel de Allende in Mexico, where the walls are covered with ornate decorations and panels – every inch celebrating with baroque details the life and death of our saviour, Jesus Christ. And there, on those richly painted walls, I came across a fantastic atlas: it showed the whole of the known world in the late 1700s. Amazing! North of San Francisco sat a great island where Spanish monks had established a monastery and a treasury, and had set aside riches for the glory of the catholic church."

"What were you doing in Mexico?" Iola asked, but clearly this was not the right question, because Ozias waved it away.

"A treasury, Iola! Did you hear me?! And I knew the shape of this coastline! I recognized it at once! That anonymous artist was directing me across two centuries to a place of forgotten riches." He tapped the paper in Argos' hand. "I scrawled down the details on the nearest bit of parchment I could find."

"This is a treasure map?" said Argos in English, somewhat breathlessly.

"I sent it to you for safe-keeping. I dared not keep it with me, in case I was robbed on the road," his uncle replied, equally breathless. "Do you not recognize it? That point? That peninsula?"

Both Iola and Argos studied the map as if it might speak to them directly, their brows crinkled with concentration.

Ozias lowered his voice, in case some craven thief was eavesdropping through the thin walls. "Don't you see? There's the knob of Ten-Mile Point, and there's the bump of Albert Head." When they continued to stare at him blankly, he threw up both hands. "Don't either of you recognize the shape of Victoria's Inner Harbour? That's the southern tip of Vancouver Island!"

Argos stared hard at it, stunned. He only saw wriggles and bumps, and that merry cartoon of a leaping fish. But if his uncle – accomplished, intelligent, scheming, and adventurous -- claimed it was Victoria, who was Argos to dispute it?

"Why would monks come here from Mexico?" Iola repeated.

"It only matters that they did, my dear sister," said Ozias in Greek, "And, with Argos' assistance, we are going to be rich!"

Ozias and Argos set out the next day. To say Iola was displeased would be a great diminishment of the truth: she was spitting mad, and she tried to reason with Ozias, but the allure of gold was too much to dissuade him with boring facts. They left immediately after breakfast with only a single leather satchel full of minimal supplies. Ozias promised, they'd purchase everything they'd need in Victoria. Iola pressed a kiss to Argos' cheek and told him to be a good boy, and do whatever his uncle asked, and not to stray from the path.

Then Ozias was away in a flap, and Argos had to hurry to catch him, and he didn't have an opportunity to ask his manoula if she meant literally or theologically.

They took the ferry across the strait, found a man who offered to drive them north as far as Sooke, then began the long hike into the mountains along an old mule path, which twisted and climbed between lines of desolate hills. The forest canopy lifted around them. They passed old log cabins left to rot, so studded with immature saplings and moss that they appeared to be wearing fuzzy green coats. One afternoon, the trail led them to a grid of dirt streets with timber buildings and fractured windows. Doors hung from broken hinges. Hearty bundles of weeds thrust up through the floors. Argos felt like they'd stumbled into an ancient ruin, but Ozias laughed at his bewilderment, and said the buildings were once a settlement called Leechtown. Men made quick fortunes here, mining gold, but isn't every boom followed by a bust? Within a year the miners and prospectors had exhausted the seams. A decade later, the town was gone. Only ghosts remained.

"They pulled out more than $100,000 of gold!" Ozias said, his eyes gleaming. They stood in the middle of the main street, flanked on either side by rubble and dross, and when the breeze blew through, it brought sounds of creaking wood and flapping canvas. "Nuggets, as big as a man's fist. Saloons, painted ladies, gunfights at noon," he continued, "It must've been like the cowboy stories of the Wild West."

"A whole town, gone," Argos said, admiring the upper balcony of an abandoned hotel. "It's hard to imagine."

"All these hills are ribboned with gold, if you know where to look," Ozias replied, shaking the scrappy map at him. "And boy, we know exactly where to look!"

They left Leechtown, heading north. That night, they slept on the open ground with a small fire between them, and Ozias told wicked stories of loose women and bank robbers as he darned one of his socks by the flickering light. Argos was enraptured, even if the tales were made more of lies than truth. As a boy, he'd spent too much time in the company of women, and he didn't know the rituals of men, so naturally, he was overjoyed that his uncle had taken him into his confidence. He thrilled to his uncle's dirty jokes, or whenever the man swore or spat on the ground. When Ozias stuck the needle into his world-worn wallet, Argos thought he'd never seen such a masculine item, and he wanted a wallet of his own, just the same.

By day, they walked. On rare occasions, they passed other men working in the woods, cutting timber or prospecting. As they followed the streams through mountain valleys, Ozias meticulously planned how they'd spend their riches, but he only spoke Greek when he broached this subject. He dared not risk any eavesdropping.

"I'll buy a big house," Ozias said, "And I'll have a housemaid and a butler. And I'll eat buttered toast and marmalade every morning for breakfast."

"I want to buy a boat," said Argos, who often dreamed of the wooden ship that brought them to Canada in 1900. "I want to sail on the ocean and visit new places, and meet as many interesting people as I can."

"I've had enough of traveling," Ozias confided. "I'm an old man, now. It's time for me to settle down, find a pretty wife, and make a brood of babies."

Argos couldn't imagine his uncle ever staying still. It seemed fundamentally wrong. Ozias Adeimantus Theos, settling down? That was as likely to happen as the entire Earth hopping off its orbit!

Then, on the second day, they paused at a rise in the road. It afforded them a good vista of the surrounding mountain peaks, and Ozias pulled the map from their pack and began to carefully examine the landscape.

For almost half an hour, he studied the map and the shape of the hills.

Then, facing due west, he said, "Aha!" so loudly that Argos jumped.

"See that?" He jabbed his finger towards one crooked peak. "Right here! Look, my boy! Look!"

To Argos, it didn't look any different from the other nameless lumps in these feral lands, but Ozias traced his finger over a line on the map – a squiggle which Argos had mistook for a trail or road. The line and the profile were the same.

They left the road and struck out across the wild ground in the direction of the hill.

The men crossed a wide river of round boulders, and climbed a series of sharp ridges covered in maple trees. That night, they slept in the woods, and it was the worst sleep Argos ever experienced. He heard small creatures rustling the dry leaves, and bigger creatures browsing at the boundary of their firelight. He imagined they'd be savaged by wolves or bears, and their holy human bodies chewed up and rendered down into animal droppings. The young man crossed himself and prayed to God that they'd survive the night, but Ozias was a true adventurer and didn't seem to care. He slept soundly and snored lustily. Argos was never so grateful to see the dawn.

The next day, Ozias progressed slowly and stopped often to consult the map. Not all of the marks made sense to Argos; his uncle had written some words in Spanish, but Argos suspected that these words might be further obfuscated by a code, because Ozias often had to work out the meaning of the words, tapping on his fingers against his skinny thigh to transpose letters.

Many miserable, swampy, mosquito-laden hours passed. Argos, already suffering from poor sleep and blistered heels, began to pray that they could soon go home, where he could eat a big bowl of his manoula's beef stiffado before rolling into bed. Treasure, be damned! At one point, he thought he spotted an immense bronze cannon half sunk in the mud, wreathed in bullrushes, but that simply could not be so. Who would drag an immense cannon so far into the wilderness? He assured himself, he was only hallucinating from a lack of food and slumber.

They walked on, but not far. As the sharp blue light of afternoon slid into the velvety gold light of evening, Ozias emitted a short gasp. Argos, a few paces behind, lifted his weary head.

"What is it?"

"Here, here, here," Ozias panted.

They stood at the base of a rocky cliff. Greenery grew tall and straight along the slope, creating a seemingly-impenetrable wall of salal and Oregon grape, tangled with horsetails and deer ferns. High up on the granite face was a strange pair of slashes. They could have been natural fissures caused by eons of ice and erosion. They could have been a cross.

The mark entranced Ozias. He stared at it, mouth agape. With quivering hands, he held up their little scrap of a map to compare symbols, then he began to giggle. Tucking the paper back into the leather satchel slung over Argos' shoulder, the old man eagerly flung his wiry body into the bushes with a whoop of joy, much like a fisherman jumps into the sea on a hot day.

The wall of foliage rustled and shivered. It must've been a few feet thick because it swallowed Ozias completely.

Argos waited, and waited, and waited.

"Uncle?" he called out, afraid. "Are you stuck?"

The cackled that emerged from the underbrush was such a wild, maniacal, bacchanal sound that Argos was *not* relieved.

Then, Ozias poked his skinny head from between the leaves, and his expression was one of utmost delight, like a boy set free at the circus. "Come along, you lazy-bones!" he beckoned, and grabbed Argos' hand, and dragged him in.

Argos half expected to hit the rock wall, but then his feet stumbled down an embankment, and he discovered himself descending a staircase cut from the living stone of the mountain. Ozias, still grasping his wrist, led him down twenty feet or more into darkness.

But the old man was a seasoned traveler, always prepared. He pulled a curious, hand-held device from their satchel and clicked it on. The battery sparked, an incandescent bulb hummed, and a beam of light cut through the gloom.

In any other situation, Argos would have been transfixed by the flashlight. Such a clever invention! But as the cave was bathed in its cool illumination, Argos felt his knees, which had never before failed him, turn to jelly.

The cavern was thirty feet high, twenty feet wide, and so long that the light beam could not reach the far end. The space was perfectly sculpted with an arched ceiling like a cathedral. The walls had been carved and shaped with great care; the chisel marks were perfectly parallel to one another, and their precision spoke of love and devotion. Numerous dark doorways branching off, left and right, into a maze of deeper chambers.

"My God," he whispered, looking up at that vast, secret sepulchre.

"This is it," said Ozias, "We've found it!" When he cackled again, the sound bounced and echoed, hinting at the cavern's remarkable depths. "Look, my boy! Look!"

Argos tore his gaze from the vaulted ceiling and dropped it to the floor, and this time, he swore not to God in florid Greek, but in a long stuttering line of nasty English curses.

The floor was paved with countless ingots of solid gold.

That night, they stayed in the cavern, protected from wild beasts by the stout stone walls. They built a little fire that only made the place seem more immense. Argos examined the carved surface, artfully chiseled, and he found words in Spanish that had been scratched into the door lintels. He pestered Ozias to translate them, but like that ancient king of Phrygia, the old man only had eyes for gold.

"There must be a million of these ingots!" he said as he pried one up and passed it to Argos. The dense weight of it was shocking.

"We'll never get them all out!"

"We'll take enough to hire men, build a trail, and rent a pack of mules," said the old man, "Then we'll come back to collect the rest, and we'll be rich, my boy! Rich as Croesus!" He continued to scheme as Argos drifted away from the fire, holding the torch, and peeked into the doorways, one after another.

The complex was a labyrinth that twisted and branched through the mountain like an ant's nest. Some of the antechambers held wooden crates, but the wood was rotten or punky, and instantly disintegrated under the strength of Argos' touch. Maybe they'd held foodstuff, centuries ago, but that had decomposed or been carted off by rats and mice. In one room he found a platform hewn from the rock. It was the perfect size for a man to sleep upon, and a cross was etched into the wall above the spot where one might rest their head. He swung the flashlight across the gravel floor. It glimmered on a bit of metal, half-buried in the pea-stones next to the bed.

There lay a golden ring.

It was tiny – an infinitesimal value compared to that boundless fortune in the main chamber – but it pulled at his heart. The ring had been fashioned into a stout band ending in two hands, clasping each other. Words etched into the band read, *'No tengo mas que dar te'*. The hands had not been fastened together. This clever design meant the ring could spring apart a little to accommodate differently-sized fingers, and Argos was able to slide it on his stubby pinky. Admiring the glitter of yellow against his nut-brown skin, his heart loved the ring immediately.

When he returned to the fire, he showed it to his uncle.

Ozias glanced at it dismissively. "Pretty," he grunted as he pried up more tiles.

"What does it mean?" said Argos.

The old man consulted the words.

"It says, 'I have nothing more to give you'. Come, boy, help me stack up a few more of these ingots, and we'll pack them in the satchel." When Ozias caught Argos admiring the ring, he gave a harsh laugh, and Argos felt shamed. After all, how could a paltry trifle like the ring hold his attention, when there was a whole treasure trove of gold ingots to salivate over?

They slept very little. Ozias was too excited. Argos found the tiled floor uncomfortable.

Eventually, he heard his uncle's breathing grow deep and steady, and the old man slumbered, dreaming dreams of a golden future. Argos folded his hands under his head to ruminate on his aching back.

But in the darkest hour of night, a sound roused him from his thoughts, and the young man rolled onto his side and lifted to one elbow.

From far away came the singing of deep voices, weaving up through the maze of corridors and caverns, no louder than the persistent drip of water on stone. He could pick individual voices from the chorale, but their words were too faint to decipher. Argos strained to hear better, and after a while, he thought he recognized the cadence of Latin.

A phantom choir, singing God's praises from the great beyond!

Were these the restless spirits of Spanish monks, long-dead and long-forgotten?

Argos had no fear of ghosts. Bears or wolves might eat him up but, to the best of his limited knowledge, no one had ever died of a spectral visitation. His heart filled with awe instead of terror. Tears gathered in his eyelashes as he listened. Laying on that unyielding metal floor with his hands clasped together in silent prayer, he gave humble thanks to Almighty God for allowing him to witness such a sacred wonder.

Then he closed his eyes to the darkness, and his thumb toyed with the gold ring on his pinky finger until, comforted, he fell asleep.

Untouched by sunlight, the two men woke late. They hurried to depart by noon.

As he packed the satchel and secured it to Argos' back, Ozias muttered 'one more ingot' many, many times. The weight grew immense. Argos complained, but Ozias laughed at him and dismissed his concern as laziness.

"You'll be fine, boy," came the brusque reply.

"I'll sink into the swamp!" Argos said.

"Don't be such a woman," Ozias spat. "You're a strong fellow! With a good spine! You'll be happy for your troubles when you're sitting on the deck of your own boat, sailing around the Strait of Georgia."

Argos kept his mind fixed on that sweet thought, and his thumb continued to toy with the ring on his pinky, but he was afraid he was going to lose it.

Every step he took, the worry increased.

Ozias badgered him to hurry, but Argos was slow under his burden of clumsy ingots, and in his fatigue, he stumbled on uneven ground. He tripped on a log. His boot caught on a stone. When he reached out to catch himself against a tree trunk, Argos feared that the ring would fly off his finger and disappear forever in the weeds.

"Wait, uncle," he called out, breath straining, "Wait for me."

"Hurry up, you lazy little shit," Ozias snapped.

Argos had never heard such sharpness in his uncle's voice. His knees wobbled and ached. Perspiration plastered his black hair to his head and ran down his brow, stinging his eyes. He tried to wipe it away with his sleeve but, again, he was afraid the sharp motion might dislodge the ring from his finger.

When he caught up with his uncle, he said, "Wait, please. I don't want to lose the ring."

Ozias flew into a rage.

"That stupid trinket!?" he howled, "One ingot could make a hundred of them! You can buy a thousand dainty pinky-rings when you're rich!"

"But –"

"Here, if you're so afraid you're going to lose it," Ozias said, fumbling in his pocket. "I'll put it somewhere it can't fall off."

He drew the darning needle from his wallet like a rapier from a scabbard.

If Argos had not been so burdened with gold, maybe he could have dodged his uncle's assault, but who could have foreseen what would happen next? Before Argos could escape, Ozias twisted up the boy's earlobe between his fingers and plunged the darning needle through the soft meat. Sharp pain burst through Argos' head. His ears roared as blood surged to the puncture. A hot spatter kissed his neck.

Ozias wrenched the ring off the pinky and, yanking and squeezing without mercy, he wrestled the band through the wound until it dangled from the swelling lobe. The tiny golden hands clasped together. The ring fastened closed.

"There, you stupid oaf," he said, "Your pretty trinket is on, good and tight. I doubt it will ever come off."

Then the old man strode into the woods, spitting and swearing. Wiping away tears and sweat and blood with his sleeve, Argos had no choice but to hurry after him, head pounding and heart aching.

They almost made it to the river when Argos unexpectedly tumbled to one knee, lurched to the left as the weight of the gold ingots pulled him over. He sprawled across the mossy ground with both hands outstretched to break his fall. He thought, at first, that his legs had collapsed from sheer exhaustion but, as he struggled to stand, the whole forest heaved and surged around him. Treetops swung wildly side-to-side, as if caught in a titanic storm.

But there was no storm. The sun blazed. The sky remained cloudless and blue. On all sides, the hills and ridges swayed and groaned. He heard the cracking of roots, the baritone rumble of landslides, and a gentle snapping that percolated under the dirt as the bedrock fractured. An earthquake! The tremors continued for almost a full five minutes, rolling up and down.

When the swaying subsided, Argos rose to his feet. He called out for his uncle.

There was no reply.

Hurrying, he gathered up the ingots and tried to swing the satchel over his shoulder, but he dropped a few into the ground where they left deep divots in the moss. Arms burdened, juggling gold bars, he scarpered through the river's cold, knee-deep water and up the opposite embankment, his shoes sliding over round, slimy stones.

Ozias sprawled beside a fallen hemlock, face down.

Argos cried out and once more dropped the satchel, rolling his uncle's limp body over, and relief flooded through him as the old man let out a wretched whimper, most assuredly alive. The awkward angle of his right calf said the leg was broken. The lump forming on the side of his head was as big as a goose egg.

"Carry out the gold and come back for me," Ozias ordered, sounding willful but weak.

Argos didn't think that was a very good idea, and he said so, but Ozias grabbed his wrist so hard that the old man's scrawny fingers left bruises.

"Listen to me, you little shit," said his uncle in a voice growing brittle with agony, "I didn't come all this way to die penniless and poverty-stricken in the mud!"

But Argos knew his uncle *would* die if he abandoned the man by the riverside. At a quick pace, it was at least a day-and-a-half's hike to the head of the trail, where he might be able to flag down a passing automobile or wagon.

Without consulting his uncle – who had regained his verve, and started to rage and foam at the mouth like a rabid dog – Argos stashed the leather satchel of gold ingots in the fresh hole made by the fallen hemlock's root pan. He covered it over with dirt, stones, and leaves, then stood back to judge his work: no one would find it if they didn't know it was here. He quickly assessed the location -- studying the shape of the distant mountains, noting the height of the sun, and finally tying his uncle's handkerchief around one of the hemlock's branches – then he slung Ozias over his broad shoulders. The pain must have been immense; Ozias' body immediately slackened and his howls stopped.

Argos ran, all day and night, until he reached the trail head. The spindly weight of his bony uncle was a fraction of the gold bars, and he made good time as he jogged onto the trail, through Leechtown's empty storefronts, then down the narrow path that followed the Sooke River, flowing like mercury in the moonlight. As dawn broke, he reached a farmhouse. A plump, middle-aged woman opened the door. She took a single glance at the wounded man and began barking orders: one child ran to a neighbour's house to phone the doctor, and another fetched water and wood for the fireplace. Ozias' skin had turned a horrible, waxy grey. His hands clenched into fists. His eyes were glazed like a blind man's. Argos was terrified.

But after the doctor came and set the leg, the woman offered them a room in the attic to sleep, and she was generous enough to let them stay as long as they required to regain their strength. Her name was, appropriately, Charity.

When Ozias woke a week later, he was inconsolable. His moods swung from lamentations to furious browbeating, and Argos was afraid to be near him. Charity was gentle and patient; she was a widow and she'd nursed her husband through his final days, so she understood that pain can turn a person cruel, even if their heart is normally loving.

But Ozias refused to forgive Argos for leaving the gold, and the satchel and -- by extension -- the map, which Ozias had tucked in the bag.

While Ozias convalesced in Charity's care, Argos hiked up the trail and back, over and over, studying the shapes of the hills and searching the wilderness for the fallen hemlock with a handkerchief tied to a branch. He never found it. By the end of September, the first wicked rainstorm slashed across the south island, and the Sooke River swelled until it burst its banks. It seemed like the whole shape of the world had shifted. Bits of the mountains had fallen in the earthquake, and friendly paths they'd followed through valleys led to dead-ends. Swamps became lakes, ridges became islands sandwiched between rivulets and creeks. Nights came earlier. When the weather turned particularly nasty, Argos sheltered in Leechtown's ruins, praying that the slanted walls could protect him from hungry cougars.

One night in late October, as an endless drizzle seeped through his sweater and dripped from his hair, Argos thought he spotted a straight dark cylinder among the pale dead reeds of a flooded meadow. The water was too deep for him to examine closer, but such a bold line rarely occurs in nature, and he realized he was looking at the barrel of that bronze cannon, which months ago he'd dismissed as a hallucination. His pulse jumped – not because he was close to the cave, which he undoubtably must be, but because the sight of something out-of-place can fill a man with dread.

Almost immediately, his shock was replaced with a flush of encouragement. Maybe he could buy back his uncle's affection! He camped that night under a nearby grove of cottonwood saplings with a tiny sputtering fire to cheer himself.

For a full week he sought any hint of their previous passage. A broken twig, a familiar stone, a friendly hollow? Nothing. With the old cannon as his starting point, he'd move across the land with great purpose, striking out towards each mountain slope in turn but, at the end of each day, he returned to the cannon defeated and empty-handed.

The hills revealed nothing.

By late-November, the weather was much too savage for Argos to hike safely in the mountains. Frost turned the rocks treacherous. The rivers were too high to cross easily, and he was afraid he'd be swept away in the frigid rapids. Upon returning to Charity's farmhouse, Argos discovered that his uncle was walking again in measured paces, guided by the encouragement of his compassionate nursemaid. When Ozias proposed to Charity in December, Argos wasn't surprised. They seemed to complement each other: Ozias told fabulous stories that entertained her children, and Charity made him laugh with her saucy jokes and steely demeanour. It took the moving of the Earth from its orbit for Ozias to settle down, but he showed no reluctance or disappointment, and slid into his new role without resistance.

Of course, he refused to forgive Argos for the rest of their lives. His opinion of the boy was so soured that it could never be repaired. When Iola moved from Vancouver to the farmhouse, Ozias berated her for bearing such a stupid son who had cursed their family to lifelong poverty. Argos felt that was very unfair – not for him, of course. He *had* been stupid. He *had* been weak. He hadn't done what his uncle demanded, and he'd lost all their gold.

But Argos felt this comment was unfair to Charity, who was patient and loving, and had shown herself to be a treasure of another kind.

On spring nights, Argos sat on the farmhouse porch and gazed towards the hills. From inside the kitchen came the happy laughter of Charity's children as Ozias sang and taught them to swear in Greek. The delicious, greasy perfume of his manoula's beef stiffado hung thickly in the fresh air. When the skies cleared of clouds and a bevy of glittering stars appeared, he thought he heard a distant choir of Spanish monks singing praise to God, and while he couldn't speak a word of Latin or Spanish, Argos understood their heavenly message. God brings treasures greater than gold to those who have the patience to see them.

The young man's fingers drifted to the ring, dangling from his punctured earlobe. *I have nothing more to give you*, it said, and Argos didn't mind at all, because he had everything he required.

Farewell: A Lion's Tale

His last morning in the mountains was a cool one. After a thunderstorm in the night, the rolling land had fallen tranquil, and the morning was almost oppressively calm; only the faint, throaty chirps of distant shore larks intermittently disturbed the peace. Overhead, the sun was a milky disc floating in an overcast sky. A series of jagged peaks shone white with a skiff of snow, but below the tree line, dark junipers dotted the rocky cliffs and cast inky blue shadows. Far below, at the base of the gorge, the thin silver line of a river snaked between spires of exposed red rock. The watercourse was so deep that it never disappeared, even in the dry season when the wind was full of Saharan grit and dusted the trees with fine sand. An ancient, gnarled ash hung over the river bank, and a gregarious crimson-winged finch scurried up and down the branches, looking for berries and buds. Other than this, the land was very still. The faint breeze was just strong enough to make the tufts of oat-grass bob their drowsy heads.

It carried a pungent odour, more like sugar than rot.

A sign of coming change.

The lionesses caught the smell and raised their golden heads, one after another, to better sample the air. The fragrance brought saliva to the tongue. They recognized the perfume immediately: a delicious gazelle.

But without need to confer, every lioness in the small pride recognized that something was amiss. Gazelles moved over the landscape in small herds. They came through this mountain pass when the earth was dusty and hot, not cool or moist. Until the sun cast off its milky coat to blaze brightly from above, the gazelles ought to be grazing farther south.

The lionesses rose from their relaxation to point their quivering noses to the west, from whence came the wind.

He was the only lion in the pride. His own aged father had died a few months back, and no other male had approached to join the group, which consisted solely of mother, grandmother, aunt and sisters. This, he supposed, meant it was *his* pride, but the lionesses still treated him with disdain. He was allowed to stay because he was young and his place had never been contested, but he rarely hunted alongside his mother.

The lionesses left the upper terrace and padded slowly down towards the river. He rose to soundless paws, shook the black mane that covered his neck and shoulders, then trailed humbly behind. He loved the tension that came from stalking prey. It created a crackling excitement in the ether, similar to the distant rumbles of thunder. What a thrill to slink through the long, whispering grasses as herbivores wandered and grazed, blissfully unaware. He hungered to move among the herd, unnoticed.

One of his sisters gave a low grunt for him to remain.

But he ignored her. He was too eager. When he continued to follow, she didn't bother to protest. The lionesses had more pressing concerns than a yearling male, trotting after them, his black tufted tail bobbing as they wound through the spires of rock.

He'd watched the matriarchs hunt many times before; he knew their habits and routines. After spotting the herd, they would target an individual -- the very old or the very young – that had fallen behind the rest. The hunters waited until the herd was a few paces ahead, then they'd circle their target like ghosts, spiralling silently closer as their lips curled and quivered. When the hapless prey browsed within striking distance, one lioness would surge forward and pounce. Powerful forelimbs wrapped around the fleeing body. Fangs plunged into the neck or, better yet, the back of the skull.

The spurt of blood and fluids.

Skinny herbivore legs crumpling.

The prey crashing into the dirt.

Then, dinner.

At the mere thought, he growled low with excitement, and his stomach growled in reply.

The strange sweet scent of the gazelle drew them forward as silently as clouds sliding across an open sky. The five lionesses slipped along the narrow slot of the gorge until it widened into a meadow, peppered with boulders that had fallen from the cliff face. Here, the river joined a second, larger watercourse. They were still in a canyon, but the sky broadened above them and the surrounding summits dropped in height: a more clement landscape, less severe than the higher reaches. The lionesses widened into a loose formation, their ears alert to the striking of delicate hooves on stones.

But he heard no such sound.

Was the gazelle alone? If so, it would make an easy and much-appreciated meal.

He kept the boulders between himself and the water, but when he peeped around the stones to the waterside, he saw the strangest sight.

Yes, the smell wafted from a gazelle, but it dangled by its hind legs from the branch of a dead tree.

How bizarre! He could barely comprehend the sight. Hanging from branches was the behaviour of a monkey, not a deer!

The lionesses were equally confused. The gazelle was clearly dead. They approached no closer, but they fanned out to the left and right, following the established instinct of circling a prey to gather valuable data.

The scent brought other predators to the riverside. From a high perch on the cliffs came the cry of a golden eagle. Bearded vultures congregated on the top of one boulder, waiting to see who would be the boldest, the first to tear the body down. A jackal skulked along opposite shore; once it spotted the lionesses, it quickly retreated and disappeared.

The young lion hung back, alone. His mother, emboldened,

approached the curious tableau with her ears pricked forward and her tongue lolling.

A sniff.

A gentle paw touched the form lightly, making it swing.

His sisters circled and scratched at the ground, trying to discern how a gazelle could find itself in such a predicament. The smell was intoxicating. The gazelle had eaten something that had altered its natural scent, and while the flesh didn't smell of sickness, it didn't smell healthy, either.

The lionesses were far ahead of him, and his curiosity overwhelmed his good sense. He wanted to poke his paw at the dead gazelle, too! He stepped out from behind the boulder and trotted down the open slope towards the shore, and for a single second, he wondered if it was wise for him to join them – if he had fallen too far behind the pride, exposed and alone.

Then his world turned upside down.

Explosions blasted down the canyon, setting off a chain of echoes that ripped into his ears and filled his head with terror. His sense of hearing would never again be keen, but that was the least of his losses. He scurried backward. The lionesses tried to dash back to the gorge but two fell almost immediately with deep wounds along their flanks, spurting arcs of blood. Maybe the others made it to the safety of the rock spires; maybe not. He'd never know.

Movement along both sides of the river converged at the dead gazelle. His nose caught the acrid, bitter scent of man.

The pride had crossed the paths of men before but, up in these lonely hills, they were always lost goatherds surrounded by puddles of delicious lamb. They always trembled or fled at the first sight of predators.

These men were neither terrified nor trembling. They surged through the river on great muscular beasts with snorting muzzles and blazing eyes. Some of the men blasted fire and smoke towards the lionesses, while others raced directly towards him, yelling and howling. He tried to retreat, but they swung knotted ropes that entangled his body and tripped his feet.

He had hung back from the lionesses and, by doing so, had made himself an easy target. As more men spotted him, he became the focus for their hunt. He circled and snapped at the nets, trying to free himself. Sharp sticks jabbed from all directions. He lashed out with bared claws but they whipped at his feet, tied up the netting tightly to bind him, until the ropes were serpents squeezing to suffocate their next meal.

One lioness dashed after the men, but she was quickly driven back by another volley of explosions. The smell of smoke filled the canyon. Chains cut into his torso. The men pulled from all directions and he couldn't dash one way or the other, but instead, remained caught in the middle of their web. He'd never felt terror before; this panic that filled his chest was a new and terrible sensation. He struggled. He thrashed. Every impulse demanded that he run, but his efforts accomplished nothing except to exhaust him completely.

He collapsed. There were cheers and cries like the squawking of birds. The net bound his limbs to his body in a most uncomfortable and undignified manner.

Unable to turn his head, all he could see was the golden eagle soaring away, into the wide milky sky above the snow-covered Atlas peaks.

They strapped him, still wriggling and snarling, to a sled dragged by a skittish brown beast. The men left the gazelle still hanging from the tree; they had no further need for poisoned meat. Their prize was won.

By dusk, the mountains and canyons lay far behind them. Long after the sun fell, they walked across a barren, rocky landscape until, eventually, they reached a cluttered, clattering, noisy collection of mud huts and stone houses that reeked of men and dogs. The procession wove through a maze of narrow alleys. People peeked out of small doorways to watch the parade pass by, their eyes wide with amazement.

The procession only stopped when they arrived in a plaza, surrounded by low-slung brick buildings and lit with guttering candles. He growled because he had no other recourse. The hunters didn't seem to know what to do with him.

But one man came running when he heard the clatter of hooves on sunbaked bricks. He threw his hands in the air, waving a stick, and hopped around like a monkey being stung by a swarm of wasps. While making inane chattering sounds, the man directed them towards a wooden cart with a crate on the back and, with much painful prodding to his rear -- as well as a dead goat that tempted his empty stomach – the lion ended up in the dark box, injured and sore and very afraid.

He did not sleep for days. His ears still rang. What little he could hear, he didn't understand. He sniffed at the holes and gaps between the boards but the smells were unfamiliar.

Eventually, the wagon stopped and the crate was pried open. Sticks poked at him between the boards until he reluctantly limped out, snarling. His legs trembled from being folded under him for too long.

The new cage was hard and unyielding. It smelled of blood and rust. Other lions had lain here; he could detect traces of ancient urine in the corners, faded with time. When he reclined, the whole contraption swayed back and forth on four large wheels, and creaked like the morning song of yellow-billed choughs. Four stout men slid the wooden crate out and another man hastily shut the door of the iron cage, and the resulting clang should have been as loud as an avalanche, but for him, it sounded muffled.

His nose remained in good working order. The air smelled of salt. The cage had been set in the middle of a large cavern with smooth grey walls, and – to his surprise -- the whole world swayed back and forth. Unfamiliar owls hooted from beyond the walls. Men wrapped in black fabric swarmed around the cage, making cooing noises. The man who jumped and chattered like a stung monkey shoved his way to the front, elbowing his companions out of the way with impatience, and pushed a hunk of fetid goat-meat through the bars.

The lion laid down and, unblinking, watched the little monkey-man. He was determined to never show weakness. He was hungry, and afraid, and grief-stricken, but a lion is ill-equipped to display these emotions. He was too proud to be prey. No matter where these monsters took him, he'd never give them the satisfaction of knowing how deeply they'd destroyed him.

"He's good and strong, just depressed," said Alphonse Moreno in polished French, slapping his wicker cane against the bars of the cage. When he smiled, there was a simian exuberance to the expression. "Don't let him fool you! He is very healthy."

The woman leaned in and studied the lion, looking deeply into its amber eyes and holding a black notebook in her slender hands. She was sleek and pretty with auburn hair and straight teeth, and her skin looked smooth and unmarred by sun or disease. Alphonse had rarely seen a woman who looked so untouched by the hardships of life. Between her beauty and her fearlessness, she seemed angelic.

But he thought as he watched her circumnavigate the cage, she was too cold and aloof to be attractive. She sucked the warmth from the room with her efficiency. When she spoke, her words came out clipped with an American accent.

"What do you call him?"

"Nero," said Alphonse.

"Like the Roman emperor?" she said, casting him a side-long smirk.

"Like the lion in Wombwell's menagerie," came the reply.

"Well, I dearly hope my employer can give this poor creature a better home than *that*," she said, "Wombwell wasn't the best at providing quality care for his beasts."

Alphonse leaned forward. "I hope you don't mind my asking, Mademoiselle Zelda," he said, "But who is your employer?"

"That's none of your concern," she replied, in such a brash and curt manner that any further questions were instantly squashed. "My employer would like to know the precise location of its capture. What was the nearest town?"

"He was caught a few miles from the pass of Tizi n'Tichka," he said, "I purchased him from some local hunters, and we sailed out from Agadir to Tangier, a week ago."

She made a note of this in her booklet.

"I know what I have," said Alphonse.

"A Barbary lion, yes," she said breezily without looking up.

Alphonse's tone lost its levity.

"Perhaps," he said, "The last to ever exist."

She lifted those dark, pretty, long-lashed eyes to him.

"There's no need to be dramatic, sir. It will not drive up the price that my employer is willing to pay."

"Ah, but perhaps Nero is priceless," said Alphonse as he waved his hand in the air. "Other parties here in Tangiers have shown interest. I've had telegrams, too, from London, Paris and Berlin. It is my suspicion that Nero is unique, as rare and precious as the mythic unicorns of old!"

Zelda snapped her booklet shut. "The Marquis of Segonzac frequently observed lions in the woods at Budaa, not far from Azrou. This one is certainly not the last."

"And how would you know what the Marquis claims?" he said quickly, without thought.

She glanced at him as if he were a bug.

"My employer..." she began, her words thick with meaning, "... knows the value of such a creature and is willing to pay you a fair price for it."

Alphonse felt his breath stick in his chest. He weighed her comment. If her employer was, truly, Marquis Édouard Marie René Bardon de Segonzac – explorer, adventurer, captain, pilot, son of a noble lineage -- then it would be of immeasurable valuable to nurture a positive relationship with that stellar figure! The Marquis travelled in elite circles in Europe, and his exploits were famous across North Africa. He enjoyed a healthy amount of political clout on both continents. Alphonse glanced at the lion in the cage and wondered, perhaps, if the sale of one mangy, skinny, tiresome, snarky, flea-bitten creature might cement a future relationship -- nay, close and personal friendship! -- with that great and influential gentleman.

"We are also prepared to offer an extra 100 francs for the cage," Zelda continued. "Given the state of the contraption, that's very generous."

Alphonse glanced at the solid iron bars, the heavy wheels, and the faded glint of gilded gold along the upper edge. This had once been ornate scrollwork, but decades of use had blunted the flowers and vines into unrecognizable humps and bumps.

"This cage was built for the menagerie of Charles III of Spain!"

"I sincerely doubt that," she replied.

"I have it on good authority, mademoiselle, that it was shipped across the Strait of Gibraltar by –"

"One hundred francs," she interrupted and made a note of the figure in her ledger. "I can pay you immediately. My employer wishes to have our dear Nero in his possession within the hour. We have already booked passage on the RMS Carpathia, and reserved a place for the beast in freight." She looked at him dead in the eye. Her gaze was as steady and confident as the lion. "This will make my employer very happy."

Alphonse pursed his lips but didn't fight any further.

A price was quickly established. Money exchanged hands. Zelda thanked him for his business, and Alphonse asked her to extend his greatest and most heart-felt gratitude to her employer. He also extended an invitation to meet her employer (preferably face-to-face, he thought, rubbing his hands together with glee) the next time their feet graced the narrow streets of Tangiers. She nodded, smiled, and made no promises.

Both lion and cage were transported to the bustling docks of Tangiers. Those amber feline eyes could not comprehend much of what they saw, but as his gaze ranged out across the undulating plains of blue water, the lion lifted his nose to the breeze and smelled salt, and fish, and smoke, and over all of it, the mingled sweat of a thousand men.

The auburn-haired woman rarely left the side of the cage. Her expression remained placid; her demeanour was watchful but cool. When they reached the busy wharf, she let forth a series of sharp commands and, almost instantly, a small army of scruffy, surly dockhands leapt to do her bidding. The cage was loaded up a narrow gangway and onto a mighty ship. The lion braced himself with wide paws and bared his fangs as the dark maw of the cargo hold swallowed him whole, but once out of the hot sun, his vision adjusted quickly.

To the woman, the hold was full of treasures – artwork, wooden crates of orange trees, statues, a motorcycle. The richness and bounty provided the same emotional effect as walking into a pharaoh's tomb. Her heart quickened. Her breath came light and lively to her throat.

But to the lion, this place was a great metal womb, where all the scents and sounds of the living world were suddenly sliced away. The familiar blue sky was replaced with inert materials, strange fragrances, and the low, unrelenting pulse of a distant engine.

The dockhands chained the cage down to bolts on the wooden floor. The woman thanked them, slipped them a few flimsy bills, then spotted a figure weaving through the stacked steamer trunks and luggage. An older lady with short snow-white hair approached, wearing a pair of khaki trousers and a flowing cream-coloured blouse. For the first time since she arrived in Tangiers, Zelda smiled.

"Look what I found, Annie!" she said as a way of introduction.

The white-haired woman was clearly thrilled.

"Is that a Barbary lion?" she gasped. She dropped the volume of her voice to a conspiratorial whisper. "I thought they were all dead!"

"Apparently not in the Western Maghreb," said Zelda, "This poor devil was pulled out of Tizi n'Tichka."

"Gosh," Annie said, her face full of delight, then with sudden sobriety, "You didn't pay more than we agreed, did you?"

"I was firm with the price, but it wasn't a problem; I had something more valuable to barter." She gave a playful wink and shimmied her hips.

Annie looked scandalized. "You didn't!"

"Of course not," Zelda corrected with a laugh. "However, I may have made a comment or two that led Alphonse Moreno to think he's curried favour with the Marquis of Segonzac."

Annie laughed uproariously. The lion flattened his ears to the crass sound, so like the harsh cries of a black kite.

When the white-haired woman composed herself, she wiped a wayward tear from her cheek. "Moreno's nose will be out of joint when he realizes his mistake. That pompous twit! He'll never talk to you again!"

"I don't plan on coming back to Tangiers," said Zelda, "And if we sell Nero for enough, maybe I can finally leave the business of brokering animals for good." She gave a wistful, longing sigh. "I could buy a little place on the California coast and be a painter. I've always dreamt of painting! Wouldn't that be nice!"

Annie crossed her arms and studied the long golden torso, knobby spine, and dry fur. "*Nero*, you called him? Well, poor pathetic Nero doesn't look so healthy."

"He just has to last as far as San Francisco," said Zelda. "Once Hearst hears that we've got a lion to sell, we'll get back our investment, ten-fold."

"Why stop at ten?" Annie laughed. "With a Barbary lion, we can name our price!"

"I hope so," said Zelda. "I'm tapped out with this one."

"So am I. Do you see me worrying? It'll be fine," Annie assured her. "My contact on Hearst's staff says the fella likes to collect art, but he's looking at adding a few exotic animals to his possessions. His ma owns a heap of land down near San Simeon, and he's thinking of building down there -- some big fancy palace or something. I don't know." She rolled her eyes. "The rich are always looking for places to blow their money." She leaned in a little closer – but not too close – to examine the lion's giant head, and he closed his crusty eyes to her. "What big shot millionaire wouldn't pay a pretty penny for a real, live lion? Mark my word, Zelda," she continued, "We draft a letter, and by the time our train rolls into San Francisco, Nero will already be sold."

"And we'll be rich."

"That's right, sister. Filthy!"

The lion gave a rattling cough, groaned in discomfort, and settled down with his muzzle on his paws. His ears still felt as if they were full of water. He couldn't determine if he was stricken by grief, or something more physical in nature. All he knew was, his head ached as much as his heart, and he only wanted the squawking people to go away, to leave him in solitude and stillness.

But still they yammered. He understood none of it. He didn't give a damn about their schemes or plans: he only wanted to sleep. He wanted to forget, if just for a little while.

"There's not many animals as exotic as a Barbary lion," Zelda said.

"Hearst is loaded, and young, and likes to stir up trouble. My contact says he's gaga for anything flashy that shows off his wealth and vitality." Her eyes widened. "He could sponsor us, to go on expedition to Mauritius and rustle him up a dodo!"

Zelda gave a derisive snort. "Not for me, thanks. If I never come back to this hemisphere again, it'll be too soon!"

They took a moment to admire the beast in the cage.

"We ought to fatten him up a bit once we get to America, don't you think?" Annie said. The first hint of concern crept into her voice. "He looks like he hasn't eaten in a week."

"Moreno says he's just depressed," said Zelda. "He'll get his appetite back once he gets used to his new accommodations."

"Are you sure?" said Annie. "I don't know…"

She might have said more, but the growl of the engines increased in strength and cut off her sentence. Cargo creaked and shifted as the mighty ship shuddered. Vibrations increased and rattled their skeletons, making the women laugh with their bird-squawks again. The entire jostling hold seemed to drift, first to starboard, then straight ahead.

"Good-bye, Africa," said Zelda, light-hearted.

The lion gave a deep and sorrowful sigh. He didn't understand the muffled sounds that the women made, back and forth to each other, and frankly, he wouldn't care about their conversation if he had. He was a lion. He had as much interest in human transactions as the business of a gazelle or the opinions of the monkey. He didn't care about millionaires or railway journeys, zoos or circuses; he had no concept of art collections or risky investments that would inevitably go wrong. The lion cared about none of it, because none of it mattered.

But as he felt the whole world around him moving, a similar sentiment to Zelda's comment drifted through his mind.

However, unlike the woman, his good-bye wasn't blithe or fond. His heart fully broke as it made a silent farewell to the continent of his blood and birth, to the land of misty sunrises and midnight thunderstorms, to the canyons where he desperately hoped the lionesses still roamed. He'd never again taste the anticipation of the hunt. He'd never see the stars rise and wheel over his beloved mountain peaks. Never again would the chirps of distant shore larks disturb his morning repose. Without any sense of what his future held, he was certain of one, all-encompassing fact.

If he could not live free, he'd rather die.

Snakes and Ladders

Right from the beginning, when she popped out of the womb a-squawlin' for the teat, a tuft of black hair grew on her chinnie-chin-chin. Her pa called her Piglet and the name stuck.

Her ma was not so pleased. Hell sure, the kid rooted and snuffled for food like a boar, and her nose was squished flat in the middle of a plump pink face, and those curly black chin hairs weren't goin' nowhere, but the woman knew a girl named Piglet was gonna have a mighty hard life ahead of her. Ma didn't know much, being the child of a West Virginia trapper, but she knew *that*.

When the doctor rolled through the hollow on his circuit six or seven months later, she asked him what sort of name would be a nice name, a pretty name, to give a little girl. As a traveling man, he'd seen all sorts of things, and he knew how to read, and he was more worldly than any other fellow Ma could hope to meet; she lived in her tar-paper shack in the hills and there weren't much opportunity for meeting a more-educated fella. As the doctor checked the baby's reactions, giving her a little pinch on the pudgy leg to see how fast she'd cry, Ma said, "The rest of 'em call her Piglet, but that can't be her name. She needs something fancy."

The doctor's route took him all through West Virginia and

Kentucky. He'd even been to Atlanta, a couple years back for the 1881 International Cotton Exposition. But, although he was plenty travelled, he'd never seen an infant with such a hairy chin, girl or boy! Still, the babe was healthy and strong in all other regards. Ten fingers, ten toes. A pair of powerful lungs. Man, she had a howl on her like a coyote! That squeaky voice reached the highest vault of heaven!

Thus, he was inspired. "What about Stella?" he said, giving the hairs a tug and getting a face full of screams in return. "It means 'star'."

"Oh, mercy!" said Ma, looking at the ugly pug of the runt. Stars twirled in Ma's eyes. "Isn't that perfect!"

And it was the perfect name, because Stella was a star, right from the beginning. She loved performing! She knew the verses to a hundred songs, she could recite poems and nursery rhymes, and she could play the spoons while dancing a jig. It seemed, anything she heard, she instantly remembered. She was like a sponge, and mercy, she loved to be watched!

But she wasn't pretty. She'd never be pretty. No one let her forget it.

Her youngest brother, Merle, loved her dearly and never paid any attention to her differences, but he didn't have a lick of sense, either.

"Stella wants to be an actress on a stage," he bragged to his friends. They were playing marbles by the outhouse, and she'd simply been walking by, intending to grab a bucket of night soil for the garden. She loved working in the garden, discovering bugs under the leaves or shooing away the little snakes so Ma wouldn't find 'em. Her heart was happy, knowing she was about to be in the midst of green and growing things, and she hadn't noticed the boys, playing. She wouldn't have walked so close, if she had.

"But she's too damn ugly!" said his friend Jimmy.

"An ugly woman should have the sense to be quiet and hide herself away," said Morty, her cousin.

Lester, her older brother, agreed. He said in her direction, "At the very least, you should pull out those god-awful curly whiskers sprouting from your chin. You got a bigger beard than Pa!"

"You are pig-ugly," said Jimmy, who was no great beauty himself.

Stella was used to being ganged-up on. Worse, she knew they were right. But damn it, she wasn't going to cry and prove it!

"At least I got my all my teeth, Jimmy," she spat.

Merle and Lester laughed. Jimmy leapt up and came at her, swinging his fists, but he missed; Pa had done a fine job of teaching her how to dodge a punch. She dashed off toward the garden, scattering their marbles with a kick as she raced by. The boys scrambled about, swearing as they tried to save their aggies.

Stella knew that wouldn't be the end of it. Jimmy was sore about his teeth, or at least the gaps where they used to be. She knew he'd want revenge: it was just a question of when. He boldly told the other boys that Stella needed to be knocked down a peg or two. She was too sassy for her own good.

Life wasn't easy in the hollow. Pa left to buy a new goat in Hillsboro and never came home. In the spring of 1902, Lester joined the army. Stella worked hard in the garden to keep them fed, and Ma was slowing down on a pair of bad knees, and after a while, the reality of Stella's situation became more fixed in her mind. She was needed here in the hollow to help run the house. It was probably best to put away her dreams of singing and storytelling on stage. What good would it do? Her beard kept growing in, thicker and thicker, and no one in their right mind would pay a nickel to see a hairy actress on the vaudeville stage! The best Stella could hope for was as much as her ma had, and that ain't much.

As summer passed, and the dreams of acting withered in her heart, Stella poured all her despair into working hard in the garden. She harvested beans. She tended the soil. She went molly mooching with her cousins, looking for mushrooms among the leaf litter in groves of elms. She liked best to stroll in the apple trees at the edge of the wood. When she plucked fruit with a basket balanced on her hip, she'd perch right at the top of the ladder and imagine standing on a stage. If she was still picking after the sun fell, she'd reach up high and hold out her hand as far as the arm would take it, hoping that her fingers might brush across the stars: her name, in lights.

One day, while standing on the top rung of the ladder and gazing at the sky, she heard the crunch of bare feet coming through the dry orchard leaves. The gaps in the branches allowed her a peek of Jimmy, strolling through the green trees, holding a little bundle coiled up in his hand. A parade of stick-limbed boys trailed after him. A few little girls tagged along, too, but they stayed at a safe distance. Stella recognized at once that this was his revenge, but she couldn't figure the precise nature of it, so she lingered halfway up the ladder. It was safer, up here. The high position gave her a little thrill of power.

"Hey there, Jimmy," she called down. "What's got your gums a-flappin' today?"

"Nothing for you," he replied, which only proved he had a trick up his sleeve, because Jimmy was the kind of boy who hungered for attention. If anyone showed Jimmy a genuine scrap of interest, he'd snap it up.

He stood at the bottom of the ladder.

"You got something there? You want to show it to me?" she replied.

"Naw, nothing for you, Piglet," he said.

The children tittered at the name.

Stella let out a weary sigh. "May as well get your tricks out of the way," she replied. "C'mon, Jimmy. Let's get it done."

"You want this?" he said.

"No, but you won't be happy 'til I do."

"Come down and get it, Piglet!"

It was a rat, she thought, or a possum baby. Either way, the poor thing was probably scared half-to-death, and liable to leap out when those cupped hands opened.

She descended two rungs on the ladder.

"You let me see it from here," she replied. "I like the view."

"Stella's a coward!" yelled her cousin Morty, "She's not coming down! Not by the hair on her chinnie-chin-chin!"

This started a chorus. *Chinnie-chin-chin. Chinnie-chin-chin.* Morty began it, but the girls picked it up and a few of the smaller ones started to dance, kicking up their dirty toes like a chorus line.

"Look, we got a piglet stuck up the ladder!" said Jimmy to his audience, and Stella's heart broke a little to see her brother Merle laughing. The chant grew louder until it bounced between the apple boughs and echoed off the clay hills to the north. Even the land and trees were teasing her.

There was no stopping this, not from up here.

Resigned and feeling loathsome, Stella crept down the ladder to face her fate.

And Jimmy, like a magician, un-cupped his hands and pulled out a length of flesh, all twisted up and twirling, and held it into Stella's face. The girls stopped their chorus to scream in horrified delight.

It was a snake.

Or, more accurate, it *had* been a snake. Now, it was a dead, crushed thing, the grey brains leaking out its cracked skull, the lifeless tail pinched between Jimmy's bony fingers. He waggled it an inch from her nose, so close she could smell the vinegar tang of its terror.

Jimmy hopped from foot to foot in his excitement. "Snake! Snake!" he said, wobbling it in front of her as the little girls shied back, squealing, and the boys egged him on.

It was dead, poor thing. He'd killed it just to make her squirm.

A ferocity bubbled up in Stella's core. Without hesitation, she twisted the snake out of Jimmy's grip and, before he had the sense to move, she slapped it full across his cheeks, leaving a sticky line of gore.

"At least I'm only ugly on the outside," she snarled in his frozen, horrified, gut-spattered face, "You're ugly, inside and out!" Once, twice, three times she slapped him across the cheeks with the snake. She would've kept going, too, but the scaly flesh gave way and the sinewy length tore in half, and Jimmy collapsed on the ground with his arms cradling his head, begging for mercy. The chorus abruptly stopped. The circle of children stared, dumb-founded and slack-jawed at this sudden shock of violence, so unlike Stella's cheerful character! Jimmy stumbled to his unsteady legs and ran for the tar-paper shacks, wiping the snake guts from his face with his shirt, and letting out a plaintive whimper from behind his fingers.

Stella, huffing and sweating, dropped the pulpy remains at the base of the tree, where that sweet little serpent could rest for all eternity.

She turned to face her audience.

The children stared back at her: a circle of skinny grubby faces, not with expressions of revulsion or disgust but of amusement and delight.

Then they started to chuckle -- at first a few, but quickly growing into a mighty roar – and their unfettered laughter filled up the orchards. Merle clapped his hands. The rest followed. The applause was so loud and rambunctious, it startled small birds from the tree tops.

The sound sparked something deep in Stella's belly. It was a dream she'd tried to kill, but some dreams refuse to die.

A smile spread across her face. Her heart thumped faster. She ran her hands through her beard, swirling her fingers through the locks and flaunting it. Why not? It was the prettiest beard to ever grace a face!

"Well," she said in her purest, clearest voice, "Once upon a time, a farmer found a snake stiff and frozen with winter's cold. He took pity on it and placed it in his shirt pocket to give it a bit of warmth. But wouldn't you know it? Once that warmth revived the snake, all its instincts fell upon it, and the snake sunk its fangs right into the farmer's tit!"

(The children all howled, just as she'd hoped!)

She continued, clasping her hands to her breast. "'Oh, mercy!' cried the farmer, 'Now I'm a-gonna die. That serves me right for pitying a scoundrel! He can't help it, 'cause it's in his nature!'" She threw her hand to her forehead and pretended to swoon, then bounced back onto the balls of her feet and hopped three rungs up the ladder, to get a better view of her adoring fans. "What's the moral of this old fable, children? Let me tell you quick! Never ever give a scrap of compassion to someone who's bitter and mean in the core of their being -- like Jimmy -- or he'll snap at you with a pair of spongy gums!"

Applause washed over her. It ignited the smouldering coals of inspiration and fanned them up into a whirling storm of fire – by all things holy, she had been born for the stage! When the doctor rolled through the hollow a few weeks later, he told her aging ma that he'd met a couple fellas in Kentucky who went by the funny name of 'Ringling'.

"I'd like to introduce you, Miss Stella," said the doctor with a twinkle in his eyes, and to her ma, he said, "I think, if we play our cards right, they might be able to make Miss Stella into a real star!"

Her ma was timid to the idea. She'd never been farther than Hillsboro, and the world is a big and frightful place. But Stella recognized a rare opportunity when it came waltzing through the hollow, and she knew, she'd be a bigger fool than Jimmy if she refused.

"Ma and I will come along," she agreed, "I'd be happy to do a little song-and-dance for your gentlemen, and see if they can give me a place in their show. After all," she said, twirling one finger through her beard and throwing him a coquettish wink, "It's in my nature."

What Walks at Barrow Lake

Orville Mann sat at the rear of the *SS Decimo's* lounge, hunched in an overstuffed chair, listening to Lou's story. His scabby hands clasped a half-empty vodka bottle on his lap. The hulking weight of the gigantic raven pushed down on his left shoulder. The bird's constant presence gave him comfort.

It was a huge creature with feathers black as sin, a hooked beak of polished ebony, and beady black eyes like jet cabochons. He'd bought the bird five years ago from a man in Vegreville, way up in the flat, boggy expanse of Northern Alberta, and that sour fella had referred to it as 'Fletcher'. Orville felt the name was too merry for such a vile, cantankerous, willful beast. No, it ought to have been called 'Asmodius' or 'Mammon' or 'Belphegor', or some other title with sinister, biblical overtures.

From their position, Orville and Fletcher scanned the crowd. On nights travelling between ports, people gathered on the *Decimo* for light entertainment, and while the hour was getting late, the crowd remained lively. The summer of 1919 had been profitable, so the mood was satisfied and smug. Every face was enraptured by the roustabout Lou Grady as he regaled them with tall tales of sinking ships. Orville, for his part, had never heard such bullshit. He took a long swig and felt the pleasing burn as the homemade vodka lashed down his gullet., When the audience clapped in appreciation, he scowled more deeply. Orville had no fondness for Lou. Neither did Fletcher, it seemed, because the raven lowered its head and let out a low, rattling croak of disgust. Both man and bird grew bitter in equal measure.

Of their growing displeasure, Lou remained ignorant. He was caught up in his own saucy tale, too deep in character to pay any attention to the peanut gallery, lurking and drinking and croaking in the corner.

The hour neared midnight. The entertainment wound down, spiralling to its inevitable close. Parents and weary children headed to bed, and at the door, Lou bid each one good-night like a tent preacher at the end of his sermon.

Orville remained seated with empty bottle in hand.

Finally, when he and Lou were the only two men left in the *Decimo's* lounge, Orville slapped his hands together slowly in sarcastic applause.

Lou cocked one hoary eyebrow in the man's direction.

"You got a problem, friend?" he said.

"I ain't your friend," Orville sneered.

"Go sleep off your liquid dinner," Lou said as he grabbed his coat and turned to leave, "I got no quarrel with you."

But before Lou exited, Orville said, "You wanna hear a *real* story?"

The old roustabout paused, one liver-speckled hand resting on the doorknob. He'd never trusted Orville Mann, the animal trainer, who cheated at poker and drank too much to be reliable. He was cruel to his animals; Lou had seen the evidence of his frightful temper, displayed as red welts across the old bear's muzzle. Most folks kept their distance from Orville Mann, not wanting trouble, but Lou's face hardened as he realized tonight, trouble had come to him.

"A story from the likes of you?" he replied. "I doubt it."

Orville stroked one scabby hand over the raven's glossy head. "It's a good 'un."

Lou hesitated but he didn't leave.

"I can't imagine you have much of a sense for stories," the old roustabout dismissed, "Is it comedy, or tragedy?"

"It's scary," Orville growled with a wicked grin. "Scarier, even, than the horseshit tale you told about the sasquatch. That might've got little

Mary riled up, but it was a bedtime story compared to mine. No, mate, my story is fucking terrifying." The gleam in his eyes was cold fire. "And made scarier 'cause it's true."

"I'll be the judge of its quality," said Lou, leaning against the wall. He didn't want to sit – that would signal agreement, giving Orville the stage – but he couldn't deny it: he was bloody curious. No one knew much about Orville's life before he'd joined the circus. This wasn't odd, in and of itself; no one spoke much about their previous incarnations. The blockhead, Argos Theos, had never divulged where he came from. Nor had the dour Dr. Kane, who curated a disturbing cabinet of curiosities, and could be just as unsettling as his pickled punks. Most enigmatic of all was the Geek, unable to speak a human tongue and devoid of all reason, confined to a filthy prison, humiliated daily, and put on display for a penny – that poor bastard! Lou wouldn't wish that dreadful existence on his worst enemy.

But Orville? He was strange. He was slimy. Stout and greasy with shifty eyes, Orville Mann was the reason Lou locked his door at night. There was a wicked wildness to him that gave Orville an aura of danger, and Lou wondered where that germ of wickedness had formed. He had a criminal's cunning, and the women whispered amongst themselves that he was an unpredictable reprobate, prone to unnatural desires. No, Lou thought, this wasn't the kind of man that's happy to work in a circus, surrounded by laughing children and colourful balloons. His demeanour was more in keeping with a pool hall, or an abattoir, or a brothel.

In Lou's unschooled opinion, Orville was the kind of man who thrived where misery abounded.

"Go on, then," Lou said, "But it's been a long day and I'm tired, so be quick about it."

Once upon a time – isn't that how all good tales start? Once upon a time, I knew a man named Jack, and Jack was a murderer.

But let me be clear. He was not a murderer in the same way as you or I would consider ourselves a murderer, if we cut a man's throat or a hung him from a tree. In the eyes of the law, yes, Jack was a murderer, but in our town, Jack's job was an important one, and he was much respected because he did what no other person dared to do. He was born in Rupert's Land more than 70 years ago, and he was already an old man when I met him, and wise! So wise. Wise beyond time.

Jack knew there is more in this world than we can see or hear. Jack was what the white fellas called a 'witch-doctor', but that title is too simplistic. Jack was a teacher and a healer. Jack knew how to taste the wind and hear the songs of the coming weather. He could whip up a poultice from moss and bark, or he could make a powerful tea to bring you back from the pox. He lived among men but he was not part of this new world; he held fast to the old ways and resisted the government's imposition. Hell, even the government agents recognized his power and authority. They never bothered him, but let him go about his work without interruption. He came and went as the seasons required.

One day, in our town, there was a woman who turned dangerous; she locked her children in the attic, raged and stormed through the bedrooms, then smashed the windows and set the beds alight. I don't remember much of it, just that the house went up in a tornado of smoke and flames, and three of her children died, and the woman laughed and danced barefoot in her yard to the sounds of their agony. The elders of the town, both white and Cree, held her down and discovered that her spirit had been stolen from her, and Jack was summoned. His strong, sinewy hands ended her misery.

Like I said, I was very young. I don't remember the details.

But when Jack came to town, he stayed at my father's house, so I was there at the dinner table when he told my father what had to be done, and he admitted he'd done that same dark deed twelve times before. Twelve murders! "More and more of 'em," he admitted to my father, his eyes haunted, "Every year, there's more."

I feared he'd do the same to me if I danced in the yard.

When I confessed this, he chuckled. 'If I do,' he said, 'You'll think it's a blessing, boy. Better to be dead than be a *wendigo*."

I didn't know this word. The names of evil things weren't spoken aloud, especially to the white folk of our town, in case the utterance caught the demons' ear and brought them to our doorstep. I was warned never to stray beyond the borders of town, but not told why – the adults had kept me blissfully unaware of the monsters that lurked in the forest. Even Jack hesitated to tell me more, but I was a pesky child and not given to respecting my elders, and eventually he caved.

As Jack told me, the *wendigoag* are supernatural giants driven by an insatiable desire for human flesh, and even though they appear starved and emaciated, they can never be satisfied, no matter how many people they consume. They're sallow and lanky, with waxy skin and glowing eyes, and their mouths brim with cruel, sharp fangs. They smell of moldy leaves and rotting teeth. They have a hissing voice, but they can mimic human speech to trick unwary travellers, and they'll creep into your campsite to steal away sleeping campers. With every meal, they grow larger and hungrier. They're cunning and clever, with a human brain that's able to plan and scheme, but they are beast-like, too; *wendigoag* move so quickly and silently over the landscape, they appear like a shadow in the corner of your eye.

A man becomes a *wendigo* in one of four ways. He might be bitten by the wendigo, or he might eat human flesh, opening his soul to possession. He might have an evil sorcerer curse him to become a wendigo, or he might dream of the wendigo, and while his spirit is walking, his physical body is filled with the wendigo's spirit, and he wakes as a monster. All these are ways that a man becomes a wendigo.

Always, the transformation is gradual. The victim grows depressed, then burns with the obsession to eat, eat, eat everything in sight. He starts to spend more time alone. He turns his back on community. Then it all curdles and he grows ravenous for the taste of men. If nothing is done, the wendigo will kill to satisfy its hunger.

"How can it be stopped?" I asked Jack with childish optimism.

"The wendigo spirit is cast out by forcing its victim to drinking hot tallow, which melts their heart of ice," said Jack. "But it only works rarely. Once they've tasted human flesh, there's no way to save them. The only way to stop a wendigo is strangle the body and burn it until no bones remain."

Lou moved to the sofa and sat with arms crossed.

"Wait a minute... this man just sauntered into town, murdered a damn woman, and everyone was fine with it?" he asked, incredulous.

"She wasn't a woman, you stupid git," Orville replied. "She was a demon that killed her own children."

Horrified, Lou stammered, "Yeah, but –"

"You gotta understand," Orville continued, "Living in isolation, surrounded by forest for hundreds of miles? If you got a problem with a person going crazy and killing babies and eating the dead, you gotta take care of it. You can't wait for the priest to show up for an exorcism, or for the Northwest Mounted Police to ride into town and start dispensing justice." He gave a snort. "Ain't that a laugh? Them, the least just of all!" Orville ran his hand over the raven's glossy head, and it let out a sound like the rattle of bones – *clk, clk, clk, clk*. He smiled as if he understood its comment, and then to Lou, he added, "A man like Jack fixes the problem before the problem spreads."

"And Jack warned, there's more of them appearing every year?"

Orville nodded.

"When my father was a small boy, there were bison all over the damn landscape," he said. "He said you could look out from the bluffs and see thousands of little dots across the open prairie, swarming like horseflies. But by the time I arrived, there were almost no bison left. You could ride a thousand miles and never spot one. They were so scarce, the sight of ten made the front page of the local newspaper!" He set the bird down on the armrest of his chair, where it hopped, then settled, then half-closed its eyes and preened its feathers. Orville ran his hand over its head. "With no bison left, folks had nothing to eat. White towns sprang up across the north and the old ways started to falter. People began to starve."

"Perfect conditions for... what did you call a bunch of them?"

"We won't speak that name again," he warned. "Didn't you hear me? Speaking the name of demons out loud brings them bastards to you."

Lou narrowed his eyes. "Fine, but –"

"Suffice it to say, I was a young man when I took a job trading furs for the Hudson's Bay Company, up in the North-West territories passed

Fort Chipewyan. Soon after I arrived in 1908, I heard the stories of a strange presence lurking in the bush, and right away, I remembered Jack's warnings. The priest said, 'don't go too close to Barrow Lake' and crossed himself for protection, but I suspected that whatever lurked there had not been made by a benevolent god. No, Lou... Barrow Lake was home to a darker force, more ancient and sinister. For the most part, the priest said I was safe in town, but I didn't know then, as I know now," Orville's lip curled up in disgust. "Evil prefers to walk among us."

I'd never seen a more congenial fella. The trapper was built like a musk-ox, wide at the shoulders and narrow at the waist, with thick red-brown hair that reached passed his shoulders, tied back with a strip of braided leather. He smiled quickly – too quick, I thought – and his expression was friendly but it wasn't deep. It stayed on the surface like a slick of oil on clear water. His smile didn't reach beyond his skin to his heart.

When he came into the post with a bundle of hides on his back, he introduced himself as Matthew Pell, and before he'd dropped that bundle to the ground, I was on guard.

"You're the new kid, hey?" he said, "Fr. Denton says you came from near Edmonton."

I just nodded and started to count hides, writing the condition of each in the ledger like I'd been shown.

"How was the road?" he continued, "Soft? Muddy?"

Most trappers were taciturn. They only came here to make their money, and they couldn't escape town fast enough once business was concluded. But this fella? He craved conversation. It struck me as odd, that someone who chose to live a remote and isolated life would be so desperate for small talk.

"Yeah," I said, "It took longer than I thought."

"Always does, this time of year," he laughed, as if he had bested me in some contest. He'd finally wrung speech out of me. I'd been broken.

"What's your name, boy?" he pushed.

"Orville," I replied reluctantly, head down, trying to do my honest work.

"I'm gonna call you Orry," he replied. "You look about the same age as my eldest son. What are ya, sixteen? Seventeen?"

"Twenty," I corrected, then pointed to the last few pelts. "Are these ones beaver or muskrat?"

"Muskrat," he replied. "I'll introduce you to my boy, next time I come to town. My wife and I got six children, but I think you and Felix will get along best." He patted his hand on the stack of furs. "It's been a good season; the trap line around Barrow Lake has been full each time I go out. I'll probably have another full haul within the week, so I'll bring him with me and introduce you."

I paused. "Barrow Lake?"

"That's right. We have a little cabin near there," he replied. "You been out that far?"

"No, sir," I said, but I remembered what the priest claimed, and looked at him with fresh eyes.

He laughed, showing two rows of square white teeth. "It doesn't feel remote once you're used to the route."

"I've heard its strange country," I replied carefully.

I expected him to correct me, but instead, he nodded. "It can be. Up there, the grizzlies are smart and they don't fear men." An eerie flame flickered behind his convivial smile. "You gotta keep your wits about you, or they'll gobble you up without a second thought."

I handed him the tally for his furs. He thanked me with a promise that we'd meet again. When he left, the temperature in the room rose a few degrees, and my pulse slowed.

Later that day, after supper and prayers, I asked Fr. Denton about the man I'd met, but as soon as I mentioned Pell's name, the priest blanched and clasped his hands together.

"A good man, most of the time," he said. "A trapper all his life. Very honest."

"Most of the time?" I pressed.

"When he and his wife squabble, he takes to drinking and it turns him miserable, but only towards himself," said the priest. "When he hasn't been drinking, he's trustworthy and honest, and on occasion, he works as a scout for the Northwest Police." He patted his hand on mine.

"You do not need to fear Matthew Pell, my boy. Not if you stay in town."

Yet, for all the priest's recommendations, there was an uncanny darkness behind Pell's friendly demeanour that I did not trust, and I resolved to avoid him in future.

This proved easier said than done. Knowing my name, he specifically requested my assistance when he visited the Company post, and if I didn't wish to incur the wrath of my boss – a snotty piss-pot from Toronto called Mr. van den Berke -- I had to keep the fur-traders content.

Mr. Pell introduced me to his son Felix. Of course we had nothing in common, but I was still polite, even if it set my teeth on edge. The boy was gregarious and over-friendly, eager to help in all ways, and constantly running every-which-way at his father's bidding. It didn't matter if the weather was sweltering or if the horseflies were biting: Felix was perpetually cheerful. The boy was astounded by the luxuries of town living, and he wanted to be pals with everyone, and most of all, he wanted to make a friend out of me. He helped load the bundles of furs for Mr. van den Berke, he helped trim the wicks of the candles in the church, he helped sweep the horse manure from the front porch of the Company with the broom that rested by the door. Always underfoot! God, it was infuriating! I hated his instant smile, his bouncing stride, his buoyant greeting. If something needed to be done, he did it merrily, regardless of whether it was his responsibility or not, and he made the rest of us look bad. Obviously, I resented him for it.

Of course, Fr. Denton encouraged this rampant civic-mindedness in the boy, because the old priest touted the values of charity and good-will towards our fellow man, and he was pleased to have a strong, young body at his disposal. The priest was too frail to care for the church. It was large, painted white and red. An alcove under the steeple held a statue of the blessed virgin, and she stared out at the town, lakes, and marshlands as if keeping an eye on naughty children. By autumn, when the weather started to turn, Felix arranged to stay at the church for one week each month. He'd scrub the floors and wax the pews, or climb a ladder and clean the birds' nests from around the virgin's feet. Fr. Denton was thrilled. Felix's fawning devotion made me hate him more. He came daily to the Company post to buy supplies or hear the latest gossip, and every time I saw his grinning, punchable face, I seethed anew.

The furs that came with the cold weather were splendid things, and Matthew Pell's furs were the thickest, plushest pelts of all. He brought in beavers, mink, wolverine, hares, and even a gigantic black bear, which he'd dug out of its den after it snuggled down to hibernate. He gave a tenth of his earnings to Fr. Denton as a tithe, so between the trading post and the church, he was the hero of the town. Women gave him gifts of pies and fabric. They asked after the health of his wife, who must be very lonely out in their distant cabin, raising all those kids. Pell thanked them and assured them, his family was quite content.

But as snow blanketed the marshlands, it became more difficult to travel over the drifts. Felix stayed for longer stretches with Fr. Denton, and the priest kept him very busy with shovelling the yard and clearing heavy snow off the roof. We saw less and less of Mr. Pell. I was happier for it.

But early one morning, before the sun rose, I heard fists banging on the door of the manse. Matthew Pell's voice howled out the name of the priest.

I sprang from my bed in the attic of the Company post and dressed quickly. The cacophony grew louder and louder, desperate and angry. By the time Mr. van den Berke and I emerged onto the street, the man was in a frothing rage. I could tell he was very drunk, stumbling in the church yard and slurring his words together. The tip of his nose was a deep cherry red: a dangerous colour for exposed flesh during a season when frostbite comes swiftly. By the time Fr. Denton opened the church door, Mr. Pell was sitting on his ass in the snow, sobbing.

"What is it, my child?" said the priest, holding his robes close around his neck to stave off the chill.

"Where's Felix?" came the strained demand. "He was due home last night, but he never arrived. Please tell me he's still here!"

Fr. Denton looked aghast. "He left yesterday morning! If he hasn't reached Barrow Lake by now, then I don't know where he might be."

This caused a fresh volley of anguish from the great man.

They assembled a search team of every brave, healthy young fellow in the town, and I knew I ought to join of my own free will, if I wanted to stay in Mr. van den Berke's good graces. We set out in a line as the sun lifted from the east, casting narrow blue shadows across the creamy white hills. Pell led the procession after Fr. Denton said a rousing prayer.

The air bit at our skin but the boggy ground was frozen solid, so we were able to make good time across the muskeg and meadows. From time to time, a small copse of trees would fracture the strong winds that swept across the open land, giving us a sheltered place to rest. We saw the tracks of wolverines and moose, but no human trail except for Mr. Pell's, which he'd left as he rushed to town.

Eventually, after hours of walking, we descended into a shallow river valley to a squat, black-timbered cabin, half-hidden under huge drifts of powdery snow. A column of smoke rose in the clear air. No one spoke.

Pell's wife was a sparse woman, her eyes wide with worry as she saw the party file down into the hollow. Our search posse broke in to smaller groups, with people striking out in different directions to cover as much ground as possible.

That was how I found myself paired with the giant Matthew Pell, heading north-east towards the shore of Barrow Lake.

He lamented his choice to live so far from town, he lamented his choice of wife, he lamented every aspect of his sorry existence, and my hatred for him grew in leaps and bounds. I assured him that Felix was not an idiot, even if (I thought to myself) the boy simpered and giggled like one. Pell thanked me for being so accommodating, and he assured me that Felix appreciated my friendship, and that I was a good man for all I'd done to help the lad.

My God, I thought, what lies had Felix told his father to foster this mistaken notion that I was, in any way, supportive? The kid had been so pudding-headed, he interpreted my sarcasm as kindness. If I'd stabbed him with a knife, he would've mistaken it for a pat on the back!

The thought made me laugh. Pell heard and agreed, it would all turn out well in the end. "We'll find him, you're right," he said, although I'd never made such a suggestion.

When the sun hit noon, we reached the south shore of Barrow Lake.

It was a God-forsaken place, little better than a marsh. The land surrounding the lake was flat and covered in a thin brown scrub. The air whipped over the ground and picked up bits of dirt, and ice crystals, and dead twigs, flinging them all into the sky with a haunting, empty moan. The lake was no wider or longer than a horse-track, but the surface was locked in place by a thick slab of blue ice, dusted with eddies of wind-blown snow.

Matthew Pell saw the lump in the middle of the lake before I did.

He let out a strangled yowl and dashed across the ice, skidding and sliding in his hurry. By the time I reached Felix's corpse, Pell had collapsed to his knees. He tried to lift his beloved eldest son into his arms, but the body was frozen to the lake and could not be budged.

Those milky, frosted eyes. Those clenched, blackened fingers. The ghostly blue pallor of his cheeks and brow. I will never forget the expression on his face, as if caught mid-scream.

The boy was naked. The legs were bent backwards and the spine was broken. I knew at once, this was not a body that had succumbed to exposure.

"Oh, merciful Jesus," I whispered, crossing myself, "What happened!?"

Then my gaze fixed on the terrible, scooped wounds across his thighs and buttocks. I clearly recognized the half-moon shapes of human teeth.

I glanced at Pell in horror.

The man ought to have been wailing. What grief-stricken parent wouldn't crumbled at the sight of a cherished son, so utterly destroyed? Instead, Pell stood as still as an iron rod, his unseeing gaze fixed on a distant point across the lake. The cherry-red of his nose was growing darker. He seemed not to care. He didn't bother to cover his face with his scarf when a fresh gust tousled his thick hair and cut across his cheeks.

"Mr. Pell!" I yelled, trying to break him from his fugue.

His blank face turned to me.

No emotion reflected in his eyes. The ever-present mask of felicity and goodwill was gone, replaced by an expression that was as flat, empty and dead as the head of one of his furs. The man stared at me unblinking as the cold wind whipped up a tornado of dry snow around us, covering the corpse of his son with a fine glittering dust. My own heart skipped a beat.

The remembered warnings of old Jack flooded my mind. I knew in that second that he was responsible.

Matthew Pell was the monster.

I swore out the word – that singular name of evil which must never be spoken aloud – and his black dead eyes suddenly flared to ravenous life, knowing that I recognized his true heart.

What could I do, but save myself? I turned on my heels and fled.

Across the scrubby land, over shallow hills and frozen patches of marsh, I ran until my chest burned and my legs cramped. Twigs snagged on my clothes and scratched at my cheeks. Daylight began to fade as the sky above filled with shifting, crackling ribbons of green light, and they swayed and pulsed as if I'd sunk to the bottom of the sea.

Then the sky clouded over and I lost my sense of direction. North became south. Looking back, I saw that my path was gently curved, not straight, and I feared I'd never find my way to civilization again. When I crested a hill, Pell's lurching form appeared not far behind, following me with his feet dragging in the snow, tracking my stumbled boot prints as easily as reading a name on a page.

I knew then that I would die as Felix had died, twisted in knots and stripped of my clothes, half-eaten by the starved beast which pursued me.

A certain terror comes with being hunted. Sometimes I heard Pell behind me, taunting me with my name, coaxing me to slow down and return to him. Sometimes his voice echoed and came from my left or my right. His unrelenting pace filled me with unimaginable dread. He'd dog me until my knees gave out. I sought protection in a grove of sapling birches, but they were spaced far apart and no thicker than my wrist, and offered no place to hide.

Again, I heard my name, again and again and again. *'Orry! Orry! Orry!'* his voice echoed over the terrain like a sob.

But Jack had warned me: the monster mimics the words of men to trick unwary victims into its clutches. From the beginning, I'd seen the falsehood of Pell's friendly nature. I trusted my gut and did not reply.

The spindly black trees moved in preternatural ways. The world shifted into a strange and wicked stage, and whether it was cold or hunger or desperation, I imagined the knobby boughs transforming into clutching fingers, reaching down to snatch me up. I stumbled from the copse into an open bog.

On a stony outcropping, not a hundred paces away, appeared the silhouette of Matthew Pell.

More craven than any man ought to be, he lurched across the landscape with his hair wild and his clothes askew, his mighty arms outstretched and his legs like the crooked hind limbs of a fox. He spat and foamed, flinging his hands out, tearing at his hair and his jacket.

I stumbled, skittered, and retreated into the trees, but he spotted me. At once he raced down from the ridge and across the bog in my direction. So quickly! So quiet! I'd never be able to escape him!

Thorns scratched at my face. Branches snagged on my clothes. Brute nature wished to offer me up as a sacrificial meal. But I persisted, and when I emerged from the other side of the grove, a faint glow tinted the clouds beyond the stunted pines. In my bumbling haste, I must be close to town.

Close to safety.

Hope renewed, I tore across open land in the direction of the lights, and as I pushed through another ribbon of brambles and reeds, I heard a new voice call out my name.

Fr. Denton stood in the middle of the snowy trail, wrapped in a black wool frock and topped with a black wool cap.

I called for him and he looked astounded as I plunged out of the bracken, into the roadway, shivering and shaking all over.

"Run, Father!" I said, "He's almost upon us!"

Fr. Denton stood like a deer, unaware of danger nipping at my heels.

"My son," he said, rooting for his crucifix around his collar. "Get behind me! I will save you!"

My breath tore at my throat. I couldn't suck in enough air to fill my collapsing lungs and grey spots swam across my field of vision. I skidded to a stop before the priest, falling hard to one knee. The whole world fell deathly still. The silence was as thick and oppressive as a blizzard.

"He's after me, father! He's after me!" I begged, clasping his black hem.

"Come, then," said Fr. Denton, "Here, let me help you, Orville, before Pell kills you, too!"

The priest's old hands gripped my wrists and dragged me after him, and a sweet relief flooded through my core. Emerging onto the trail was Pell's figure, outlined by the moon, racing towards us.

But I was with God now, and safe.

Suddenly, a lance of ice pierced my neck. My whole body went rigid with shock. The blood in my veins froze, burned, churned and coursed, spattering across the white snow – red and white, the same colours as the church. I released a howl of confusion and agony.

Pell, farther along the track, leapt towards the sound of my pain.

I managed to turn my head a few scant degrees, and I saw the old priest's mouth latched onto the exposed flesh between my scarf and my jacket, his skinny throat undulating as he gulped feverishly, suckling at the essence which coursed through my veins. I struggled but he held me fast. I could not dislodge him, no matter how I flung my arms or kicked out my legs. The core of my body was pulling out through the wound in my neck, like a sock turned inside out, and I was barely aware of myself for the pain. I had just enough sense left to realize the error of the Father's comment – how could Fr. Denton have known that Felix was murdered, if the old priest had not seen the body himself?

Then Pell's square fist descended from the sky, breaking the priest's hold on me. Dislodged, Fr. Denton sprawled across the road. His thick black slug of a tongue lashed across his wicked fangs and bloodied chin.

Pell kicked me out of the way with no kindness. He fastened his meat-slab hands around Denton's sickly neck and squeezed the life from him just as Jack had done, so many years before. I saw things then that I have never been able to rectify. The priest's face contorted, the purple lips pulled back, the long-pointed teeth snapped at Pell's determined face and, in one burst, bit off the blackened tip of his nose. Pell was too focused on holding Denton down to notice the wound. They struggled together, churning up the snow and the dirt and the blood, until it was a mire of boot marks, gravel and gore.

At last, Denton crumpled and lay still.

Pell demanded I carry the body into town, and he stared openly at the oozing injury on the side of my neck, keeping his distance from both of us.

"Jesus Christ!" Lou exclaimed.

"They burned Fr. Denton's body in the churchyard," Orville continued. "Elders were summoned from the surrounding villages, and they tied me to a cot and waited to see if the monster had possessed me. For three miserable weeks, old women sat in shifts and watched me without a scrap of empathy. My wrists were raw from the bindings. I musta pissed that bed a hundred times."

"But you healed? You were alright?"

Orville gave a half-hearted shrug, pulling down the collar of his shirt to expose a wicked, puckered, half-moon scar. "When the elders agreed that I was still a mortal man, they let me go." Orville looked sour. "But the damage to my reputation was done. Word spread far and wide that I'd been bitten by that wretched demon, and it was only a matter of time before I turned into something sinister and unholy. I wasn't surprised when Mr. van der Berke released me from employment with the company; he knew no one would trade with me. I was useless to him. No matter where I went – Rupert's Land, North West Territories, Yukon, Alaska -- I'd be a pariah."

"And that's why you came south?"

"I joined the Canadian army and went off to war with the rest of the poor unfortunate rabble," Orville continued. "When I came back, no one gave a shit about monsters anymore. I mean, hell, we'd seen monsters all over the goddamn place!" He shrugged. "Jack wasn't wrong when he said they were multiplying, but with the new century, they started taking different forms. They possessed people to do all sorts of unspeakable acts against their sisters and brothers, and the victims were left to fester in the trenches and the madhouses." He replaced his collar and held out his hand. With a snap of his fingers, the raven hopped onto his forearm.

"That's one helluva tale, Orville," Lou said with skepticism.

"Believe me or not. I don't give a toss," said the man as he tottered unsteadily to his feet. "You keep telling your silly little ghost stories and fairytales, but know that some of us have seen those forces with our own two eyes, and they ain't nothing to laugh at OR fuck with. You hear me, Lou?" He leaned in close. Lou smelt alcohol on his breath and, deep behind it, the stench of blood and rotten flesh. "Truth needs to be given the respect it deserves."

Orville Mann hobbled out of the *Decimo*'s lounge. Before the door slammed shut, Fletcher gave one final caw.

For a long time, Lou leaned against the railing of the starboard deck, looking out at the wrinkling sea and smoking a cheap cigarette to calm his nerves. The world appeared a little bigger than before. It contained shadows he'd never noticed. He wondered if a man can ever be fully healed when he's witnessed such unimaginable horrors and escaped with a psyche so terribly scarred.

And that night, when he retired to his berth to sleep an uneasy slumber, Lou locked his door and, for good measure, wedged a chair under the knob.

Forever Underground

Cards slapped down on the table in quick succession. Each man groaned or grinned according to the whims of Fate revealed.

"Two pair, aces and kings," said Hugo, only fourteen years old. He was losing badly but he didn't much care. The opportunity to play cribbage with adults was worth the price of his meagre earnings.

The men swapped amused smirks. They might have tried to scam anyone else, but Hugo had two marks in his favour that kept him from becoming an easy mark: one, he was a likeable young fellow, eager to please and full of good humour, and two, he was the son of the boss. They played fair with Hugo, but they didn't make it easy for him.

"Morgan's Orchard," said Farley, one of the circus roustabouts. "Peg up your four points!"

Hugo looked confused as he moved his ivory marker on the hand-carved board. "What?"

The other players chuckled. Toot Simmons leaned forward. The old boilerman was missing most of his teeth and his smile was like a bottomless chasm, black as the ace of spades. "Back in the old country, a fella named Morgan owned fruit orchards in Kent, and he'd regularly run his barges down the Thames to market in London. The company symbol on the barges was two pears." He tapped one yellow fingernail against the cards. "That's what you got there: two pairs."

"My turn," said Bud Pritt. He was the captain of the *SS Decimo*, and he had a gruff and gravelly manner that hid a compassionate interior. He wore a peak cap and a wool vest, both of humble brown wool, faded and patched from years of wear in the open weather. "15-2, 15-4,15-6,15-8, and two is 10." The mariner gave a gravelly, self-satisfied laugh and rubbed his hands together with glee.

They watched him take his allotted points. His ivory piece raced far ahead of anyone else.

"Damn it, Captain," said Farley, "You're gonna wipe the table with us all."

"Have a little charity for the kid!" said Toot.

But Bud smirked at Hugo. "How are you gonna get better, if you don't challenge yourself against the best?"

There was good-natured ribbing, glasses refreshed, a few remarks about the little brass bowl of money next to the cribbage board. The pot wasn't big tonight, only 2 dollars, but still -- that amount could buy a man a new pair of boots.

"You just learned your first lesson, kid," said Toot to Hugo, "Never play cribbage against the captain."

Farley counted out his pegs, glancing at Bud. "I heard you won your first boat in a card game. That true?"

"A little wooden dory named *Christobel*," Bud replied. "She was falling apart at the crossbeams, but yep, I won her playing poker in Steveston."

"How old were you?" said Hugo.

"Twenty-two," Bud replied. "I'd been fishing on the *Stalwart* for a few years, and figured I knew enough to strike out on my own."

Toot sat back in his chair. He was losing badly and in no hurry to continue the game. "Twenty-two? Isn't that a bit old to be starting out with your own boat?" He glanced to Hugo. "My pops first took me to sea when I was seven, and my brother had his first boat when he was sixteen."

Bud took a swig of rum. "I didn't start out fishing. I was the first in my family to make a living on the ocean. Yeah, I suppose you could say, I got a late start."

Hugo leaned forward. "What did your father do?"

"Coal mining," Bud replied. "He was a miner in Cumbria, before making his way to Pennsylvania, then out here to Nanaimo."

Toot counted his cards and moved his marker. "I never pegged you for a miner's son."

Bud removed his peak cap and set it on the table, then scrubbed his hand through his thinning brown hair. "I started working in the mines when I was nine, on the picking table. My old man was able to move me quick into underground work in Number One – money was better. I helped with the mules, loaded carts, ran errands and the like."

Both Farley and Hugo found this passably interesting, but Toot paused. The younger men didn't seem to know or care, but Toot was similar in age to Bud, and he was clever, too, and he knew his history. "Number One?"

"That's right."

"After? Or... before?"

Bud blinked slowly. "Before."

Toot gave a low whistle. "Crikey!"

The two younger men glanced up from their cards. The mood in the room had suddenly dropped.

"You knew men lost in the explosion?" Toot asked.

Hugo glanced at Bud, to judge his reaction, but the captain remained calm and cool.

"Many. My father included."

"How old –"

"Fourteen," he interrupted Toot. "Same age as Hugo, here."

Toot let out a huff. "Holy hell. I'm sorry to hear it. That must've been a kick in the nuts."

Bud laughed at that. "Yeah. I suppose you could say that."

"There was an explosion?" said Hugo.

"It musta been a bit of luck that you weren't working that day," said Toot. "The angels were looking out for you!"

Bud took a moment to savour his mouthful of rum. Then, after some consideration, he said, "The angels were looking out for me, true, but I worked that day. I was there when it happened."

Toot lowered his hands to his lap. "How --?"

"You already said it," Bud replied, "Divine providence. I was saved by the grace of God, and I'll never forget it."

The younger men now stared hard at him. "What happened?" said Hugo, for he was too young to have the weight of experience on him, and he didn't know not to ask.

The captain took another swig of rum. "Do you know much about Nanaimo's history, laddie?"

Hugo shrugged one skinny shoulder. "It's a fun place to perform. They have good crowds. Dad says they like to give up their money, so it's always profitable – not like New West or Vancouver, where folks hold their wallets a little tighter. Nanaimo enjoys a good show and they're appreciative of the circus."

All of this was true and Bud nodded slowly. "Nanaimo is a solid town. Good, honest people. I figure that's because it's built on coal mining," said the captain, "The work pays well enough, but it a hard job and dangerous, too. You come to appreciate the good things in life." He reclined in his seat. "There's nothing that quite compares to a shift in a mine, though. When you're down underground, you can hear the gas hissing out of the stones, and in Number One mine – which burrowed out under the ocean – you could hear the engines of the boats passing overhead."

Hugo sickened a little at the thought. His face turned a bit green.

"That would give me the willies," he said.

"I liked it, at first," Bud continued, "I started going underground in January 1887, and that particular winter was wickedly cold, so working in the mine was warm and sheltered from the wind. It was better than the picking table! And I made more, too, to bring home to mother. Mining is satisfying work; you can physically see what you've done during your shift, how much you've dug out, how much farther along the wall you've moved. Yes, it's plenty satisfying." He softened with the memory. "But it's plenty dangerous, too, and I didn't know any better. When I started my shift on May 3, 1887, it felt like any other shift. I went down the shaft without a care in the world." Bud took another long drink. "What did I know? I was fourteen years old."

Four of us were on the face that day: my father, Mitch, Bagsy, and me in the back. Mitch worked the drills, Pa and Bagsy had the shovels and loaded the barrow. I just held the light and kept the water coming, to keep the dust down. The roof was low. We'd worked this same small seam for almost a week, no more than three feet high, creeping away from the main shaft as we followed the black rock through the grey. We were all bent over at our waists with crooked knees, breathing each other's sweat, teasing Bagsy for all the garlic he'd eaten or the pungent tobacco he chewed.

No one ever talks about the smell in a mine. The air gets close and still, and nothing moves, so smells pool and fester like pond-water. You've got the stink of the men you're with, and you can pick out all the hints of their life above ground, like what their wives cooked or what they ate in the bunkhouse, or what their stomach disagrees with. You could smell the manure from the horse in their yard, or the soft apples that have fallen under their trees, or the seaweed from the beach if they'd been crabbing.

Then there's the coal itself. I can still remember the smell of it : the clean, acidic, vinegar scent of a fresh rock face, or the gritty dry musk of an old seam, or the pale lemon-and-salt fragrance that clings to chunks of quartz. Some of the old timers would lick rocks, too, claiming you can tell all sorts of things from the taste of a stone. Not me, though. I could smell the movements of the seams around us, and I liked the rocks' ancient perfume. They didn't fart or belch. They didn't stink of cholera or crusty runs. The rocks were old and pure and stable and unsurprising, and I loved them.

No. 1 Mine had a shaft 600-feet deep, and once you reached the bottom, you had to walk level for a little before the seam sloped down, spreading out in a web of tunnels under Nanaimo Harbour. A few tunnels even stretched out under the channel to Protection Island. The coal was good and plentiful, and the pay was generous – my pa made almost $4 a day, which was a princely sum. I made a little less, on account of being a boy, but every bit helped the family, and we were grateful for it.

As I said, we were working the front of the seam, to the north of the main slope and two right turns off the main shaft in a small pocket. The labour was hard but straight-forward. Pa drilled the rock, Bagsy tapped in a bit of black powder, then secured a fuse into the hole by tamping in a plug of moist, crushed coal. That would direct the blast forward into the seam, instead of back at us.

Once the wall was blasted, we'd move along the face and gather up the chunks of black coal, shovelling pieces into a wooden wheelbarrow. When the barrow was full, I pushed it out to the larger shaft where a mule and mine-cart waited. I dumped the contents and pushed the empty, bouncing barrow back to the face to start all over again. That was the job, and I did it well, ten hours a day.

A Chinese fella waited with the mule. The foreman called him 'Wong Ling', but the white miners called him 'Jimmy', and when I shared half my sandwich with him, he said I could call him 'Kee'. I asked him how he kept everything straight with all these folks calling him different things, but he said Wong Ling was not his name: it was only his paper name, used on the documents he'd shown to get the job. The real Wong Ling was a decrepit old fella who'd sold the documents to him for a very good price, and having papers gave him the ability to work for the Vancouver Coal Company. As for the name Jimmy, that was just a diminutive nickname, and not exactly spoken with kindness. Kee, however, was what his mother called him in Guangzhou, and he knew in his heart who he really was. That's all that mattered.

I called him Kee, and he called me Buddy, and that worked fine between us.

When the mine-cart was full, Kee led the mule out to the main shaft, where he'd dump the load into a coal-car, which would then be pulled by rattling chains to the surface. Then Kee returned to our team, down through the maze of narrowing tunnels.

On that May morning, he was in fine spirits. I was, too. It was pay day for the miners, and on the surface, the fresh air held the promise of summer. We both had plans that put a spring in our step. For me, it was my mother's birthday, and after my shift, there would be cake and cut flowers on the table, and plenty of card games with friends and neighbours. Kee, on the other hand, planned to buy a new pair of shoes. Normally he sent his earnings home to his sister in China, but Kee had met a pretty young lady, and he wanted to look his best when he went calling on her tomorrow night. He needed to make a good impression, and his battered boots just wouldn't do.

Bagsy was in high spirits, too, but in a way that was unkind. He always teased Kee ferociously, but on this day, he seemed to have a bullheaded nature about him, and he wouldn't let up with the insults. Pa told him three times to knock it off, but Bagsy wouldn't. Sometimes a man gets his knickers in a twist and he needs to take it out on a person; the target could've just as easily been me, as I was the youngest in the hole, but Bagsy didn't like anyone different from him. He chose to focus his venom on Kee.

Mitch warned Bagsy to cut it out – that's when you know it's bad, 'cause Mitch never said boo to anybody! But Bagsy persisted. He dumped coal on the narrow-gauge tracks; Kee had to shovel it off, or else the mule couldn't pull the cart. He pinched the mule's nose; Kee almost got kicked. He said cruel things, he mocked and teased. He threatened to tell the foreman that Kee was a lazy good-for-nothing and have his pay docked; Kee ground his teeth but kept his head down. I felt sick about it all. Kee just had to take it, because he if he didn't, he'd lose his job.

This went on for a couple of hours. I noticed Kee getting red in the face. Every time I brought a barrow out to the cart, Bagsy would follow and hassle me with all the ways I did my job wrong, and then at the cart, he'd pinch and pester. Finally, he crossed a line. I don't know exactly what, but Kee snapped. He wasn't having none of it anymore.

Kee threatened to punch Bagsy in the nose. I said I'd help.

When Bagsy retreated back down our side-shaft, scurrying like a crab and whining that he ain't done nothing wrong, Kee followed.

There were shouts between them. There was shoving. I tried to stay back but there wasn't much room to avoid it! Pa told Mitch to get a foreman. Mitch hustled out to fetch help when Bagsy picked up a shovel and threatened to kill Kee. Lord, it was awful!

But they were too busy shouting to hear the groan in the rock. I heard it. Then I smelled it too: a sudden current of peaty, whiskey-scented air that pushed into the side-shaft and made my ears pop.

Everything happened fast. The rock floor became as supple as a wave on the surface of the water. High up in the wider shaft, the mule let out a scream. I felt a thud pulse through my bones, like the flat of a hand slapping my back. I heard metal pings and pops as the rails bent and the spikes flew. Then the whole tunnel tipped upside-down and I crashed against the wall, shitting my pants. Everything went black. I never heard the first explosion, but damn, I heard the second. As I lay in the darkness on a bed of broken coal, it ripped through the main shaft, roaring like a freight train. The mule screamed again, then silence.

But the roof of our side-shaft collapsed at the entrance, and that cobbled wall of quartz and granite and shale saved us from the force of the blast. Me, Pa, Bagsy and Kee: four men, trapped in a pocket of air, almost a thousand feet underground.

My first animal instinct was nothing but *get out*. The rock fall ensured that weren't gonna happen. I patted my chest to make sure I was alive, and sucking in desperate breaths as my mind whirled. I was afraid to light the Davy lamp but I couldn't smell gas. After an hour or so, Pa said was better to die suddenly in another explosion than linger in this nightmarish dark. His voice was very small. I'd never heard him sound so afraid. I searched the ground until I found our equipment. Bagsy's lamp was busted. So was Pa's. Mine worked and gave a small flicker of illumination.

Bagsy's leg was crushed below the thigh. Kee was all scrapes and bruises, but his limbs were whole. Pa was the worst: he was pinned down between two boulders, and no amount of leverage with the shovels could budge them. Kee and I worked as Bagsy cursed us and shouted slurs, but Pa told us to leave and find ourselves a way out.

But there was none. The shaft was sealed shut.

Pa died a few hours later. It was awful. I don't think about it, ever.

Bagsy persisted. His leg was an oozing mess! We were forced to listen to him howl out his anger, trapped in a tiny pit only five feet wide, twelve feet long, and three feet high. The smell of blood and terror made the whole place stink like a butcher shop. I cried for the loss of Pa, and

Kee cried, too, and goddamn Bagsy teased him for it. Even in the midst of hell, that man couldn't let up. We crouched together in our own coffin and he didn't have the strength to be a decent!

Kee suggested I turn off the light to save oil. We waited another hour, sitting and praying. In the syrupy dark, I heard a sudden struggle and Bagsy cry out for help, and then I heard a gurgle like a kitchen sink, emptying. I smelled blood again, but this time, the copper fragrance was fresh and lively.

I hurried to re-light the lamp. Bagsy's body lay in a fetal position below the coal face. A heavy chunk of quartz had fallen on his head and crushed it to pulp.

The thing was, even down in the pit of hell, I knew there was no quartz near the face. I kept the face clean for the miners, moved the spoil away with my own bare hands, and I was good at my job. The only quartz in sight had been a few stray chunks that had tumbled loose from the spoil tip at the entrance to the side-shaft, a good ten or twelve feet away from Bagsy. In the flickering lamplight, I stared hard at the glittering white chunk embedded in his mangled skull, covered in splotches of red and grey.

Kee crouched near the body. He wore an expression I'd never before seen: half-way between resignation and relief. I know now, with the benefit of experience, that it was the look of a man preparing to die.

"I'll never say a word," I promised, "Bagsy had it coming."

"Don't matter none," he replied.

"He died in the fall. I'll back you up."

Kee shrugged. "I won't need those new shoes now."

"The draegers are coming," I assured him.

"I'm sorry about your pa," Kee replied. "Nice that you'll be buried together, though. You're with family."

"The draegers are coming," I repeated.

My exhausted mind went around and around, like a dog chasing its tail. I couldn't think of anything to say, so I said it again.

"The draegers are coming, Kee."

"No," he said softly, "They aren't coming for us."

His tiny voice was inconsequential against the massive weight of rock, bearing down on us on all sides. Despair filled me up like a cup of cold spring water. For the first time, I knew without question that my life was done.

Kee and I sat together in the gloom and heard the groaning rocks. I picked out the distant whir of a motor on a fishing boat far above us, and I desperately wished I was standing on the deck of that ship, exposed to the sweet air and the friendly sea.

Kee used his finger to write a few characters in the dust on Bagsy's shovel. I asked him what the symbols meant.

"It's my real name," he replied, "When they find us, I want them to know who I was."

Then he cried, and so did I.

We waited for a long time, an eternity, as the little flame in the Davy lamp danced and twirled. We waited for the air to run out. Neither of us had been injured badly. Suffocation would claim us. We just had to be patient.

But the light didn't go out.

And we didn't die.

Kee was the first to realize the implications of that. "I think," he began slowly, not wanting to get his hopes up, "I think there's air getting in."

"Yeah? You think so?"

He nodded.

I held up the Davy lamp to the rock fall and moved it along the surface of the stones. The flame bobbed merrily, then suddenly flared brighter. I smelled it, too: the scent of cold smoke, drifting in with the air.

"Here," I said quickly.

He snatched up a shovel and together we beavered at the rocks, using the lever to tumble them down, seeking passage. At last, we'd opened a way through – not big enough for a man, but wide enough for an arm. Outside, the main shaft was black and charred. Our little lamp threw barely enough light for me to discern the burned remains of the mule and the half-full mine-cart, tipped on one side, wooden slats broken.

Bagsy's shirt was wet with blood, so I unbuttoned Pa's shirt and slid it off his grey body. I wadded up the dusty fabric, tying the sleeves into a knot. It was filthy with coal and oil – highly flammable. I lit a few loose threads with the lamp and they flared like a wick, then I tossed it through the passage, onto the cart's shattered timbers. Kee and I took turns peeking through the hole, watching the flames rise, watching the orange light grow and spread along the charred shaft. Greasy smoke billowed. Instinctually, I was afraid the smoke would fill the outer chamber and choke us... but what did it matter? We were already corpses, just waiting for our turn to rot.

But it never filled the room. It flowed up and along the slope of the ceiling, rising and roiling. It became a living thing, seeking escape.

Then Kee heard the sounds of rhythmic banging, and together we called out, over and over. We sang a song together. Our throats were dry and our voices cracked, but we kept singing. Eventually the flames began to shrink but it didn't matter; as the main shaft darkened, cold electric lights came bobbing through the gloom, and I heard men calling out to us, trying to triangulate our location.

A blackened, sooty, coal-shrouded figure in a helmet and goggles appeared through the smoke. He yelled, "Here! Here!" Footsteps came running.

Then there were five of them, with shovels and poles, pulling out the rocks to free us. Kee pushed me forward and the draegermen seized my wrists, and they pulled me through the passage like a midwife yanks a babe from the womb. Then they pulled out Kee. He and I clung to each other as the men urged us to hurry, even though we were exhausted and half-blind from coal dust and smoke. The draegermen were at our heels, barking orders to go *faster, faster, faster*. We ran until our lungs ached and our knees howled.

I did not know, until much later, that fire had swept through the lowest levels. Management demanded that the tunnels be flooded, or else the company risked losing the whole operation. Our little pocket of air was far beyond the line of explosion, in a zone where no one should have survived, and the draegermen had been in the process of retreating to the surface when they saw the glow of our little fire. They craned their ears to the narrow tunnel far down the main shaft, and heard the distant echoes of our desperate singing.

Within the hour of our rescue, the company flooded the tunnels. A million gallons of sea water, washing and frothing down into the dark abyss.

I don't like to think too deeply on it.

Almost as soon as we reached the surface, Kee and I went our separate ways: he was taken to the Chinese quarter, and I was taken to the Nanaimo Hospital, and because I never knew his real name, I never saw him again. That pains me most. For a whole day in a dark tomb, we clung together and kept each other sane. We emerged like butterflies from a single cocoon -- completely changed by the experience. He'd become my brother. But once we were rescued, no one told me what happened to him. I'll never know. The only fact of which I can be sure is, he's alive the same as me, and I must remain satisfied with that.

All the cards were on the table. No one cared much about the cribbage board anymore.

After a moment of respectful silence, Farley let out a foul curse and laughed, "I don't believe it! You're pulling our legs."

Bud took another swig of rum and said nothing, but glanced at Hugo and rolled his eyes.

Toots crossed his arms. "They say the company lost 150 men that day."

"Only seven survived," Bud replied.

Hugo stared wide-eyed at the captain. "I don't blame you for never going underground again! I couldn't stand it!"

Bud threw the boy a smirk, full of camaraderie and good-humour, which helped cover up the dregs of fear that simmered within him. On those rare occasions when he thought of the disaster, he struggled to suppress them completely.

"In my darkest moment when I realized, I was going to die, I'd heard the ships on the surface. The ocean called me to her. Once I left the Nanaimo Hospital, I promised myself that I'd abandon the coal miner's life forever, no matter how much money a man can make swinging a pickaxe. I headed straight for the docks, took a scummy job on the first fishing boat I saw, and never looked back." He glanced over the cards in his hand. "When I won that old wooden dory, I changed the name from *Christobel* to *Lucky Kee*. It seemed like the proper thing to do."

"You're a good captain, too," Hugo replied. "You take to it natural, like you were born to it. I've never seen you shirk in the face of a storm."

Bud slapped his cards down on the table. "I don't care how wicked the storm is, or how high the waves are! They'll always be better than the stale air, the groaning rocks, and the smell of coal dust. No, laddie, I refuse to have rocks over my head again." He counted out his points, which took his peg all the way across the finish line. "When I die, Hugo, don't bury me in the soil of a churchyard. Bind me in linen and throw me overboard, so I can float on the waves until the angels find me." Then the captain took the brass bowl of money, emptied it, and claimed the winnings for himself. "Better that, my friends, than forever underground."

The Cat and the Karluk

Grover Scott was 4-feet 2-inches of ruthless, scheming, simmering fury, and while he made a very shrewd circus owner and a no-nonsense boss, Lou Grady knew it was never a good idea to stay on the dwarf's bad side. Grover wrote the paycheques. Grover owned the boats. If you wanted to stay in a cushy position in the Circus Salmagundi, you needed to stay in his good graces.

Most folks might think a job as a circus roustabout is hard on the body, but Lou Grady figured it was the sweetest gig he'd ever had. He'd been a ship's crewman all his life, and at sixty-three years old, Lou favoured the idea of sailing towards his golden years in a comfortable managerial position. That's how he saw himself: a manager. The performers thought he was a roustabout, the land-dwellers called him as a scallywag, but he'd accrued enough seniority to order the younger men around, and he never had to lift a finger to raise the Big Top. These wiry grey hairs garnered him a bit of respect. He played his fiddle, and he told his stories, and children came to him for advice and penny-candies. Yes, Lou very much appreciated his position in the circus, and he didn't want to lose it. It was in his own best interest to keep Grover happy.

As much as one could, of course. Grover was quick to anger. For someone who dressed as a clown on opening nights, Grover sure could be a miserable curmudgeon.

Since telling the story of the *SS Clallam*, Lou had experienced a certain frostiness from his employer. Two months had passed and Grover had made it clear, he didn't want to hear any more tales of maritime disasters. When people gathered for a tale or two, Grover had actively suggested stories from the other roustabouts and, to Lou, it looked like Eddie Sunshine might soon usurp his place as the troupe's raconteur.

That would not do. Not for Lou.

So early one evening in April 1920, as the Circus Salmagundi was preparing to leave its winter quarters in Cedar-by-the-Sea, Lou made a point of asking Grover -- to his face -- if there was anything the old man could do to make amends and return to his former position of storyteller.

"I thought my cold shoulder was bugging ya," said Grover with a smirk.

The two men stood together on the aft deck of the *SS Nona*, and watched over the railing as people brought luggage and supplies on board. The voyage would only take them as far as Esquimalt, but it was the first show of the season, and folks were noticeably excited.

"Your daughter didn't like the story about the *SS Clallam*?" asked Lou, already knowing the answer.

"Poor Mary didn't sleep for a month," Grover replied. "What the hell were you thinking?"

"My pa told me worse stories when I was a lad," he replied.

"You and Mary aren't cut from the same cloth," Grover scoffed.

"Maybe not," Lou replied, "But she's not squishy, either. That girl's got a strength in her that hasn't come out yet... but when it does?" He let out a whoop of a laugh. "Aren't you gonna be surprised!" He jabbed one bony finger towards Grover. "And you can't tell me that the rest of the group didn't find the story interesting."

Grover scowled. "It *was* a good story."

"You can't keep a true artist down, Mr. Scott," Lou replied. "Would you tell Gertie not to ride on her fine horses? Or tell Bill not to throw knives at Wanda? Or tell that new lady, Rosie What's-her-face, to cover up all her tattoos? Of course you wouldn't. And yet you do that very thing to me! You're purposefully silencing me from telling my tales – a service that I generously provide free-of-charge to keep your employees happily entertained." He slapped one hand to the centre of his chest. "Sir, I am being suppressed!"

Grover rolled his eyes.

"God damn, Lou," he said. "I am not suppressing–"

"I have been censored!" Lou continued. "Boxed up and locked away! Put out to pasture in my prime!"

"Jesus," Grover growled, "Is telling stories really this damn important to you? Fine. You get one more chance. But I swear, if you scare my kid again…"

"Children are stronger than you think," Lou said. "And I have just the story to prove it."

That night, after dinner, those who were not plum-worn out by packing the boats gathered together in the lounge of the *SS Decimo*. It was a mellow crowd. Many of the adults had been made drowsy and pliable with bathtub gin. A friendly little fire burned in the iron wood-stove in the corner of the room, and soft couches with plenty of pillows lined the walls. Lou took his place at the front of the audience, and he saw many friendly and eager faces: Bill and Wanda, the knife-throwers, cuddled together under a patchwork quilt. Tall, lean Dr. Kane reclined against the back wall, smoking his pipe. Pretty and petite Gertie, the trick-riding acrobat, sat on the couch with a cup of hot cocoa in her hands. Next to her was Mary Scott, Grover's little girl. Her expression was stony, and cautious, and brimming with suspicion.

"How are you tonight, Mary?" said Lou.

"Fine, at the moment," she replied back. She was a mite of a thing, only 9-years-old, but the hard set of her mouth was steely. Her words contained an unmistakable tone of warning. "You gonna tell us another scary story, Mr. Grady?"

"It has some suspense," he said. That earned a nervous chuckle from the group.

"Suspense is okay," she clarified, "Sinking ships ain't."

"Oh, dear! Then I might be in some trouble," he replied with a cheery grin. "Have you ever heard of the *Karluk*?"

Her dark brows drew together. "No."

"Not many know about the Karluk Expedition," he started, "And I'll be honest, it's a harrowing account of starvation, heartache, and horror, but there's triumph, too, and a couple of strong-willed kids, and," His smile widened. "The toughest cat you'll ever meet in all of Canadian history."

Lou felt heartened, for with the mention of the cat, her wary expression shifted to curiosity. She leaned forward a little.

"You got a story about a cat?"

"Yes, I do," he replied, brassy and bold. Lou raised his chin and faced the crowd, and looking straight at Grover, he said, "I'm gonna tell you about the cat and the *Karluk*."

Back in 1884, Matthew Turner's shipyard in Benicia, California, built a fine brigantine named *Karluk*, which is the Aleut word for "fish". She was 129-feet long and powered by both sail and a 150-horse power auxiliary coal-fired compound steam engine, and while she appeared to be sound and strong, her engine -- from the very beginning -- was never very powerful. It was described by her engineer as a "coffee pot of an engine...never intended to run more than two days at a time."

For a few years, she lived a happy life as a fish boat, but in 1892, *Karluk* was converted for use as a whaler. Her bows and sides were sheathed with two inches of Australian ironwood, which is dense, exceptionally hard, and too tough for termites to chew. All decked out in her armour, she completed fourteen whaling trips, with the last one in 1911.

Then, in 1913, *Karluk* was purchased by a man named Vilhjalmur Stefansson for the bargain price of $10,000. He had high hopes for the vessel, but his ambitions and expectations were more than she could bear. She looked strong, but she was about to be tested through the ferocious onslaught of an Arctic winter, and that was a trial she wouldn't survive.

But first, let me tell you a little about Vilhjalmur. He was a Canadian explorer and ethnologist, born to Icelandic parents in Gimli, Manitoba in 1879. He was a fancy fella, a graduate of Harvard, and after doing some archaeology in Iceland in '04 and '05, he went north to the Mackenzie Delta and lived with the Inuit during the winter '06. By God, Stefansson loved the north! In 1908, he and an Inuk guide named Natkusiak undertook an ethnological survey of the Central Arctic coasts of the shores of North America, and for four long years, they worked for the American Museum of Natural History, writing down all they could about the folks that live in those cold, icy lands.

When they were done, Stefansson immediately began planning another expedition to the high Arctic, approaching the National Geographic Society and the American Museum of Natural History for financial backing. They were happy to oblige, but Stefansson was an ambitious fella, and he wanted to explore the Beaufort Sea, too. At the time, the area hadn't been well-documented; Stefansson wanted to change that, and discover new islands to fill in the blank parts of the map. For such an endeavour, he needed more money, so he approached the Canadian government.

Canada, Norway and the United States were all seeking claims of sovereignty over the high Arctic. The Canadian government feared that an American-financed expedition would give the US a legal claim to any new land discovered in the Beaufort Sea, so Prime Minister Robert Borden met Stefansson in Ottawa in February 1913. Borden hoped that the expedition would strengthen Canada's claim over the Arctic islands, so the Canadian government offered to assume all financial responsibility for the entire three-year expedition. The American sponsors agreed to withdraw, but the National Geographic Society placed a condition: if Stefansson failed to depart by June 1913, the Society would reclaim its rights to the expedition, thereby nullifying the Canadian deal and losing Stefansson his additional funding.

It was a narrow deadline. Stefansson had only a few months to prepare. He needed to hire crew, organize research, gather supplies, and buy ships – no small feat! He used three ships: the *Mary Sachs*, the

Alaska, and *Karluk*. The three ships would rendezvous at an old whaling station at Herschel Island, off the Canadian Arctic coast, where they would divide up equipment and supplies. It was also on Herschel Island that Stefansson would divide the group into two parties: a Northern Party to search for new islands, and a Southern Party to carry out anthropological studies.

The expedition's scientific team included representatives from Denmark, France, Norway, the United States, and the British Empire. They were distinguished men in their fields, but most had no experience in polar exploration. Only Alistair Forbes Mackay, the expedition's medical officer, and James Murray, the oceanographer, had previous experience: they'd both been on Sir Ernest Shackleton's *Nimrod* expedition to Antarctica between '07 to '09. Other scientists included William Laird McKinlay, a young science teacher from Glasgow, and Bjarn Mamen, a skiing champion from Norway who would act as the expedition's forester, even though he had no scientific background.

Thirty-six-year-old Robert Bartlett had already captained a ship to within 150 miles of the North Pole, so he was experienced in polar navigation. He'd recently returned to Brigus, Newfoundland from the spring seal hunt when he received a telegram from Stefansson that he'd been hired as the captain of *Karluk*, so he rushed west to British Columbia to join the expedition. This meant that he lacked sufficient time to select a crew, so he haphazardly picked sailors from around the dockyards in Victoria before setting sail. They weren't exactly the cream of the crop; McKinlay wrote that one crew member was a drug addict, one suffered from venereal disease, and (despite alcohol being forbidden on board) the crew had smuggled plenty of liquor onto the ships. They also brought a little black cat.

On June 17, *Karluk* left port in Victoria, BC to sail north, but in the weeks leading up to their departure, Stefansson had mostly been absent, and he'd only revealed a few details of his plans to his team. Expedition members worried that in their hurry to meet the National Geographic Society's deadline, they'd sacrificed the quality of their food, clothing and equipment.

Stefansson dismissed their concerns, accusing them of being "impertinent and disloyal". The expedition's departure was such a mess that the men and equipment were loaded onto the wrong ships. Disputes began over the chain of command, too. The Canadian Geological Survey had provided four scientists to the expedition, and it wanted those men to report directly to the agency rather than to the expedition leader. Stefansson didn't like at all. To make matters worse, Stefansson lay claim to the publication rights of all private expedition journals, and the leader of the Southern Party, zoologist Rudolph Anderson, threatened to resign if unable to take credit for his own work.

Right from the start, Bartlett doubted the *Karluk's* seaworthiness. He saw that she hadn't been built to withstand the pressures of ice on her hull, nor did she have an engine strong enough to punch through sea ice. But there were other, more pressing concerns: the engine needed constant attention, and the steering gear was unreliable at best. By the time they reached Nome, Alaska, the men were spitting mad about the whole affair. They demanded a meeting with Stefansson to clarify plans and sort out the equipment. Stefansson dismissed their concerns. God, the men were angry, but even though they threatened to quit, none of them did.

At Port Clarence, north of Nome, they brought 28 dogs on board, then continued to head north towards their rendezvous point on Hershel Island. On July 28, the ships crossed the Arctic Circle, and on July 31, *Karluk* reached Point Hope, where two Inuit hunters known as "Jerry" and "Jimmy" joined them. On August 1, they spotted permanent ice pack. For a whole day, *Karluk* tried to thrust into the ice. Finally, she punched through, but that sense of accomplishment was immediately lost: *Karluk* became trapped, and she drifted eastward for three days before reaching open water again.

While the *Karluk* was stuck, Stefansson travelled over the ice to Point Barrow and brought back a trapper, Jack Hadley, who became the ship's carpenter. Soon after that, at Cape Smythe, two more Inuit hunters, Keraluk and Kataktovik, joined the expedition. They also brought with them Keraluk's family—his wife Keruk and their two daughters, Qagguluk and Mugpi. Qagguluk was 8-years-old. Mugpi was only three.

The protective brass plates on Karluk's bow were damaged, and Captain Bartlett was anxious about tangling with ice. He tried to follow channels of open water, and over the next few days, *Karluk* struggled to make headway. Bartlett was forced to take the ship away from the coast. By August 13, Bartlett calculated their position as 235 miles east of Point Barrow, with a similar distance to travel to their rendezvous point at Herschel Island, but despite his best efforts, *Karluk* would go no further east. The ship became firmly stuck. Trapped in the shifting ice, she began to move slowly westward and, by September 10, they abandoned any hope of reaching Herschel Island in time to meet the *Mary Sachs* and the *Alaska*. *Karluk*, and all on board, would have to winter where she was.

After a week, they started to run out of meat. Realizing the boat might be stuck for a good long while, Stefansson announced that he would lead a small hunting party over the ice to land and search for game. He promised to be back in ten days. He took Jimmy and Jerry, the expedition secretary Burt McConnell, photographer George Wilkins, and anthropologist Diamond Jenness. Before they left, Stefansson instructed Captain Bartlett that, should the ship start to move again, he must send a party ashore and construct beacons with information about their direction.

But on September 23, a blizzard struck the ship. The ice floe in which *Karluk* was trapped began to drift. Soon she was moving between 30 and 60 miles a day, westward and away from the hunting party. Bartlett, trapped on the boat, quickly realized that Stefansson would never find his way back to the *Karluk*.

The snow, the fog, the poor weather, all conspired to make it impossible for Bartlett to calculate where they'd gone. As they began to head north and away from land, he feared that the *Karluk* would be crushed by increasingly thick ice. Desperate, he ordered supplies and equipment to be moved off the ship. Not only would this help to lighten the *Karluk*, but it also meant they could escape quickly if she broke into pieces and sank. The crew hunted for seals to supplement their food supplies, and by mid-November, their drift shifted south-west, towards Siberia. Even in these bleak conditions, they decided to celebrate Christmas with presents, decorations, and a banquet, but their merriment was short-lived: by New Year's Day, the ice began to buckle into pressure ridges, cracking and drumming with loud, ominous bangs.

On January 10, 1914, early in the morning, a tremor shook the whole ship. Bartlett gave orders to remove snow from the decks, hoping to lighten the boat and raise her up above the crushing ice, but he also ordered all hands to dress warmly and prepare for the worst. At 6:45 that night, a roar erupted under their feet. Ice punctured the hull. Water rushed in through a huge crack. Barlett gave the order to abandon ship. Through driving snow and darkness, the crew hurried to move rations and supplies, and Barlett remained on board for *Karluk's* last moments. He put Chopin's Funeral March on the ship's Victrola, and the music echoed out across the barren, frozen landscape as he stepped off the ship to join the others.

Within minutes, crushed and twisted, deck planks snapping and ironwood armor cracking, *Karluk* disappeared through a hole and was swallowed by the sea.

Left stranded on the ice were 22 men, one woman, two children, 16 dogs, and the little black cat.

A heavy, oppressive silence filled the lounge of the *Decimo*. When she spoke, Mary's voice sounded small and fragile.

"Is that the end?"

"Of the *Karluk*?" asked Lou. "I'm afraid so."

"But is it the end of the story, too?" she pressed.

Lou shook his head. "Of course not! There's lots of story left."

"You said this was the story of the *Karluk*, but this story can't be about the ship," she explained, "Not if the ship has sunk to the bottom of the ocean."

"Oh, Mary," he replied with a little shake of his head. "A ship is more than just a bunch of wood, hammered together and floating on the ocean! A ship is the people who live aboard, and sail her, and keep her safe, don't you think?"

Mary narrowed her eyes. "I guess."

"The ship is just the body; the people who sail aboard her are the soul," he replied, striking the centre of his chest. "And yes, the Karluk's body sunk to the bottom of the sea, but haven't we all been taught, the soul is a holy thing, and even after death, it persists…"

They called it 'Shipwreck Camp'. It was comprised of a few small shelters, built of canvas or packing crates. In *Karluk's* last minutes, they'd managed to save the stove, and there was plenty to eat, so Captain Bartlett remained hopeful. He knew they could last a while on the ice.

But he knew, too, that eventually they'd need to strike out for Wrangell Island, a round dollop of treeless rock that rises out of the Chukchi Sea, 90 miles north of mainland Siberia. Oval-shaped and only 75 miles at its widest point, Wrangell Island consists of a southern coastal plain, a central belt of low mountains, and a northern coastal plain populated by polar bears, puffins and musk ox. In the depths of mid-winter, it's shrouded in perpetual darkness, the snow-blown slopes illuminated by the unholy green glow of the Aurora Borealis. Bartlett was not yet willing to trade the comforts of Shipwreck Camp for the stability of solid land. It made more sense to wait, and use the last week of January to slowly gather their strength and prepare their gear as the days lengthened into February.

But Mackay and Murray - both of whom had been on Shackleton's Antarctica expedition - and the anthropologist Henri Beuchat were dissatisfied with the idea of waiting. The men argued to leave as soon as possible. Captain Bartlett was persuaded to send a small, fast-moving advance group to prepare a camp, and on January 21, a small party struck out for Wrangell Island. The group was led by *Karluk's* first officer Alexander Anderson, and included crew members Charles Barker, John Brady and Edmund Golightly. Bjarn Mamen would act as a scout. They were given instructions to set up a camp near Berry Point on the north shore of Wrangell Island.

On February 4, Mamen returned to Shipwreck Camp. He'd injured his knee and left the group just as they spotted land, but he figured it was probably Herald Island, not Wrangell.

Captain Bartlett sent a second team to establish the exact location of this island, and to determine if Anderson's group had actually succeeded in reaching it. The ship's steward Ernest Chafe, along with Kataktovik and Keraluk, came within 2 miles of Herald Island, but a channel of open water prevented them from reaching it. They looked through binoculars for any sign of the missing party, but saw nothing.

Meanwhile, on February 4, Mackay, Murray and Beuchat, along with crewman Stanley Morris, announced they were leaving the next day to strike out for land, too. Captain Bartlett knew he'd never persuade this third group to stay, so he gave them a sled, a tent, six gallons of oil, a rifle, ammunition, and enough food to last for fifty days.

Looking across the open channel with their binoculars, Chafe and the second team concluded that Anderson's company hadn't reached the island. The second team returned to Shipwreck Camp, but they crossed paths with Mackay's party, and found them struggling to travel across the ice. Mackay's group had lost some of their provisions and clothing. They'd even discarded some of their heavier equipment. Beuchat, delirious and raving, suffered from hypothermia. Chafe offered assistance but the third party refused to return to Shipwreck Camp. They struggled on their way, never to be seen again.

The only hint of their fate was Morris' scarf, later found buried in an ice floe. As for Anderson's party, they disappeared, too.

"Will they ever be found?"

Mary sounded worried.

Lou glanced at Grover. The dwarf wore a fearsome scowl.

"I imagine they will, as folks press out into the map and explore," said Lou quickly, trying to soothe every concerned heart. "It's only been a decade since they vanished. Perhaps Anderson's group safely crossed the channel to Herald Island, and made a snug camp, and --" He stumbled, knowing this loose thread of the story might be a little too unsettling for his employer's liking.

"I don't like the thought of never being found," Mary replied. "It makes me feel all queasy in my belly."

Gertie wrapped her arms around the wee girl. "Let's imagine that they were rescued by Russian fishermen and transported to Siberia, where they married plump Siberian wives and had lots of rowdy children," she chirped. "Isn't that a much better end to their story?"

"Of course it is," Dr. Kane agreed, sounding sarcastic, "They loved their new lives so much, they forgot all about their old lives, and never wrote a single letter home."

Mary cast him a sarcastic glance. "I'd rather imagine they *survived*, Dr. Kane. You can imagine a tangle of frozen skeletons in a canvas tent, if that's what you prefer."

"Fine, fine, make up the rest of their story, however you wish," said the doctor, dismissing her with a flap of his long hand, "Everyone gets a happy ending." Then, turning to Lou, he said, "Continue, Mr. Grady – tell us what happens to the rest of them."

The remaining group at Shipwreck Camp now consisted of seventeen individuals: Captain Bartlett, engineers John Munro and Robert Williamson, sailors Hugh Williams and Fred Maurer, fireman George Breddy, cook Robert Templeman, the trapper John Hadley and Henri Chafe. There were also the scientists McKinlay, Mamen and George Malloch, Keraluk's family of four, Kataktovik, and the little black cat.

Despite the harsh conditions and hardship, three-year-old Mugpi was a jolly and spirited girl, and her antics became a source of joy and distraction for the group. At one point, her father, in despair over their situation, wondered aloud if they'd survive the year, and Mugpi replied cheerfully that they were alive now, and that was proof enough that they were going to keep on living.

The weather improved, the days grew longer. When February arrived, Bartlett decided it was time to strike out for solid land. He knew that most of the party was inexperienced with travelling over ice, and it was going to be a demanding, perilous journey, so he sent small groups out to blaze a trail and to lay down supply depots. When, at last, they were ready to leave Shipwreck Camp for good, Bartlett divided the survivors into four teams. The first two teams left on February 19, and Bartlett led the last two groups on February 24.

Travel was strenuous. The surface of the ice thrust upwards into fierce peaks, broken and jagged, sharp as glass. Storms swept away sections of the blazed trail. Keruk carried Mugpi on her back, while Qagguluk helped her father with the sleds. On February 28, they were stopped by a series of tall ridges, some reaching as high as 100 feet straight upwards, that stretched in a giant wall east and west as far as the eye could see. The men slowly chopped their way through the ridges. Three turned back to Shipwreck Camp to pick up a few more supplies, but when they returned to the main party a week later, the group had only advanced three miles.

Those three miles were the worst they'd experienced, but after they crossed the last of the ridges, the ice became smoother again and much easier to cross. On March 12, utterly exhausted, they reached the northern shore of Wrangell Island.

Now on solid land, Bartlett took stock of their situation. A few men were injured. Many suffered from frostbite. All were weak from their journey. He'd originally thought they could rest at Wrangell before continuing on to the mainland, but the captain realized that the group would never make it. He ordered them to set up camps around the island, most likely to give the bickering men space. Then, Bartlett and Kataktovik continued on alone.

By April 4, the two men reached the Siberian coast. Soon after, they found a small village, where they were given food and shelter by the local Chuckchi people. Then, heading southward again, they moved down the coast from village to village, through blizzards and bitterly cold temperatures. On April 24, they reached Keniskun, a small trading station on the Cape Dezhnev peninsula. It had taken them thirty-seven days to travel 700 miles.

In Keniskun, Bartlett met a man named Mr. Caraieff, who had been a graduate of a college in Vladivostock and spoke English. He informed Bartlett that the ice in the Bering Strait was breaking up, so there was no way to take a sled back across it, but nor could they take a boat until later in the season when the icebergs were gone. "If it's too dangerous to use either boat or sled to get back to the North American side," said Bartlett, "Then we should head south to the larger town of Anadyr, to send a wireless message to Ottawa."

Mr. Caraieff felt this wasn't a good plan, either: the melting rivers would make the roads impassable, and besides, there was no guarantee that the wireless would be working when he got there.

Instead, Mr. Caraieff introduced Barlett to the Russian Supervisor of Northeastern Siberia, a distinguished gentleman named Baron Kleist, who offered to take Bartlett to Emma Harbour, a larger center located about a week away. Here, the captain would be able to find a larger ship to take him back to Alaska. Bartlett said goodbye to Kataktovik and, on May 10, set off with the baron by dogsled. Six days later, they reached Emma Harbour. Five days after that, Bartlett boarded a whaler and journeyed back to Nome. Ice prevented him from landing there, so instead, Bartlett continued to St. Michael, where he finally sent a message to Ottawa. As soon as he told them of *Karluk's* fate, he began searching for a rescue vessel to save the stranded party.

Back on Wrangel Island, things were not going well. Just as Bartlett suggested, the survivors had set up individual camps at locations around the island, but almost as soon as the captain left, dissension seeped through the group. Food supplies dwindled. Hunger set in, and people accused each other of hoarding supplies. McKinlay wrote, "The misery and desperation of our situation multiplied every weakness, every quirk of personality, every flaw in character, a thousandfold."

Injuries were plenty. Chafe's feet became gangrenous after severe frostbite, so Williamson clipped off his toes with improvised tools. Malloch's frostbitten feet refused to heal, and Mamen's dislocated knee gave him constant pain. To make matters worse, a strange sickness began to affect members of the party; their legs swelled and they grew too exhausted to move. When Malloch died on May 17, Mamen was too ill to bury him, so the body lay in the tent for days until McKinlay arrived to help. Ten days later, Mamen died, too, of the same mysterious disease.

"What killed 'em?"

The question came, not from Mary, but from one of the brawny crewmen sitting at the back of the lounge. At first, Lou didn't recognize Eddie Sunshine's voice: the man was a hearty, experienced traveler, and he'd lived on ships for most of his life, working as a deckhand on many long-haul voyages. The timidity of his words was out-of-place. It immediately belayed his fears.

"I don't think anyone knows," Lou answered.

"The swelling legs, the fatigue – we had something similar strike the crew on a trip along the Argentinian coast," said Eddie, "At first, we thought it was because of the cold and the frost. It claimed a few before we figured out, it was a sickness in the pemmican."

Mary turned in her seat to speak directly to him. "What's pemmican?"

"It's a kind of travelling food," Eddie explained to the girl, "You dry red meat -- usually bison, venison, beef, moose, caribou, most anything'll do -- and grind it into a powder. Then, it's mixed with an equal amount of melted fat, and sometimes berries are added to make it taste sweeter." Eddie patted his stomach. "Lots of fat, lots of protein. It'll give a man energy without taking too much space in the cargo hold."

Dr. Kane, lingering and listening with only half-an-ear, perked up. "Did you say, high-protein, high-fat?"

"That's right," Eddie replied.

Kane puffed on his pipe as he considered the information. "The human body has no mechanism for storing protein like it does for fat. If a man has excess protein in the blood, eventually it causes kidney damage."

"Maybe the pemmican wasn't made right," said Mary.

Eddie nodded. "Lou said Stefansson was in a hurry to purchase supplies at the beginning of the expedition. Maybe he wasn't paying attention to the quality of his ship's rations."

"If the pemmican made for Stefansson's expedition didn't contain enough fat, then the men were consuming too much protein for their bodies to process," Kane agreed. "Given their symptoms, it sounds possible that they died of nephritis."

"Ain't that a fancy word! Maybe so," said Lou, "I only know the story, not the science." He turned to Mary. "Your father only gives us good healthy food on these boats, so you never need to worry about that."

"Good," she replied. "Because this story is only getting worse, the farther we go."

"Every story has to get bad before it gets better," Lou replied, and he took a steadying breath before he continued, knowing that the worst was yet to come.

Wrangell is the summer breeding ground for birds like snow geese and terns, and in early June, birds began to appear. These provided a much-needed source of food, both meat and eggs. You'd think, with the days growing longer and food available, that everyone would be in better spirits, but the meat and eggs became a new reason for endless bickering and conflicts. Nasty accusations of hoarding were slung around the group. McKinley lost a few items and wondered if someone had stolen them. Williamson suspected that Breddy and Chafe were thieving.

On June 25, a gunshot blasted through the silent Arctic air.

They found Breddy dead in his tent. It may have been an accident while cleaning his gun, or he may have been driving to suicide, but the trapper Hadley claimed it was murder, and he cast his wary eye towards Williamson. Panicking that they'd all turn on him, Williamson proclaimed his innocence and claimed that Hadley's suspicions were hallucinations and absolutely untrue. Between starvation, desperation, and despair, who can say what had actually happened? The verdict was never determined, although a few of McKinley's stolen items were eventually found, stashed in Breddy's camp.

All in all, the castaways were miserable, hungry, and hopeless. The survivors raised a Canadian flag on Dominion Day, attempting to bring a little levity and celebration to their plight. It did no good. By August, without a hint of rescue, the destitute party began to prepare for another ferocious Arctic winter.

But on the morning of September 7, a ship's whistle rang out across the island. Mugpi was the first to see the *King and Winge*, an American-registered schooner, a quarter of a mile off shore. On board was Burt McConnell, Stefansson's erstwhile secretary, who had been alerted to the survivors' location by Bartlett in Nome. By afternoon, all fourteen survivors had been taken aboard.

"They were saved?" Mary asked.
"Yep!" Lou replied.
"The cat, too?"
"Yes," he assured, "Even the cat."
"Oh, thank goodness!" The girl let out a grateful sigh and collapsed against Gertie.

Glancing to the back of the lounge, Lou was very pleased to see Grover, stony-faced as always, but with one corner of his mouth turned up in satisfaction.

Captain Bartlett was criticized by an admiralty commission for taking *Karluk* into the ice and allowing Mackay's party to leave, but he was also publicly hailed as a hero and honoured for outstanding bravery by the Royal Geographical Society.

Stefansson, however, was privately critical of Bartlett, and Bartlett was just as unimpressed with Stefansson. After leaving the *Karluk* group, Stefansson and his group of hunters reached the mainland but, when they discovered the ship was gone, they continued back along the Arctic coast. In Stefansson's opinion, the crew of *Karluk* were never in any grave danger: after all, they had provisions for five years. There was nothing else he could do for them, and he was ambitious man, driven to complete his work. Within a few months, he purchased the schooner *North Star,* gathered new supplies and a new crew, and continued to explore the north. By March 1914, around the same time that the survivors were reaching Wrangell Island, Stefansson visited the Southern Party, which was excavating an old Inuit settlement on Barter Island. He seemed indifferent to the plight of his lost crew and, believing the discovery of new land was more important than science or safety, Stefansson continued his search for new islands. When he returned in

1918, he proudly claimed to have discovered three. He was honoured by the National Geographic Society and given the presidency of the Explorers Club in New York, but in Canada? His reception wasn't so warm. The expedition had been costly, both in money and human lives.

Keraluk, Keruk and their two daughters, Qagguluk and Mugpi, returned to their home at Point Barrow. Mugpi came through the ordeal with only a single injury: one day, after chasing the cat, it had lashed out at her and left her with a scratch on her chin.

An appreciative silence descended over the crowd. Lou paused, signifying that his tale was at its end, before turning to Mary.

"Well? How was that story, miss?" he pressed, "Was it better than tales about sasquatches and sheep?"

"Much better, Mr. Grady," she agreed, "I prefer stories where at least *some* of the characters survive."

"I'll keep that in mind for future," he promised.

When he glanced at Grover, his employer gave him a pert nod. Yes, there would be future stories allowed. Lou felt a great relief.

But as he took his seat by the stove, Mary's little brow furrowed. "But Mr. Grady, what ever happened to the cat?"

"Oh, well!" he laughed, taking up his own mug of ale. "She was adopted by the crewman Fred Maurer, and taken home to his family to New Philadelphia, Ohio." He grinned widely. "Fred's a cousin of mine. We write letters back and forth; he told me about his time on the *Karluk*, and it mustn't have been so bad, for he's signed up with Stefansson's next expedition to Wrangell Island, leaving this September. Ain't that just like Fred! He can't say no to a good adventure!" Lou took a long sip to parch his dry throat. "I can assure you, Mary, that the cat is living a very comfortable life on land. Last I heard, she'd even had a litter of kittens — all black, but with feet and bibs as white as Arctic snow."

The Business of Flesh and Blood

The sway of the passenger carriage and the rhythm of the wheels might have rocked him to sleep, if his heart hadn't ached so dreadfully. The pain in his chest was worse than his hands, and that's saying something.

A hundred dollars from his father and a kiss on the cheek from his mother: that's all they'd given him before putting him on the first westward train. He was warned, never return. His mother wept but turned away when he tried to comfort her. The disappointment in his father's eyes was enough to tear him apart. It would have been better if he'd died in Belgium. Preferably at the hands of the Germans, of course, but he suspected that his parents would have been content if his own attempt had been a success, too. Suicide is a sin, sure, but then they could've told their friends and neighbours that he'd died in the Great War. His memory would bring pride to the family, and no one would ever be the wiser.

But he'd lived, damn it. He'd failed.

And that failure only compounded his father's shame. Weak of character, frail in spirit, with hands left trembling from fright, and now? Not even competent enough to take his own life.

Hector Kane pressed his temple to the cold glass of the carriage window. The train had pulled out of Montreal three days ago, on the morning of April 12, 1917. In that short amount of time, the landscape had transformed from quaint villages and granite hills to marshland and prairie, but he didn't care. Kane closed his eyes to the world spinning by.

"Y'alright, fella?"

Yanked from his thoughts, he opened his eyes to a stout, middle-aged man dressed in his Sunday best.

"Quite," he replied in a tone that betrayed, he was not.

The man hesitated. "D'ya mind if I sit here, 'cross from you?" He gestured to the empty seat, facing Kane.

Kane waved his hand towards the seat as a gesture of acceptance.

The man sat quickly, afraid that the welcome would be rescinded. "Thanks," he said, "I'm traveling with my eldest brother. He can be a real pismire, when the mood strikes."

Kane returned his gaze outside.

But the man, with a certain nervous tremor to his voice, continued. "I told him, I ain't playing another round of rummy – that's all we been doin' since leaving Regina! I just want a bit of peace. Isn't that what all men want? He wasn't happy with that, oh no, and I figured, best if I just leave him be, and seek out my quietude elsewhere!"

"Of course," Kane replied without taking his eyes from the land.

"Gosh, beautiful country, ain't it!" the man replied. He thrust one calloused hand out. "I'm George Hatch. And you are?"

"Dr. Hector Kane." The offered hand was shaken but, when Kane reached over, his sleeve pulled up and exposed his wrist. The skin was pink and hairless from the bandages. He quickly withdrew and pulled it down.

"Nice ta meetcha, sir," said George. If he noticed, he said nothing. "I'm going as far as Calgary. I live down in Okotoks – a short ride, but it'll feel like a long one, if my brother is still in a mood. How about you? Going to Calgary?"

Kane saw no escape from conversation. "I'm afraid not."

"Vancouver, then?"

He gave a belly-deep sigh. "To be honest, Mr. Hatch, I'm a man without a destination. I need to find work, but I'm not sure if Calgary or Vancouver are suited to me."

"I'd figure there'd be plenty of work for a doctor," said Hatch.

"Ah, there's the trick," said Kane. "My hands give me trouble. A most regrettable condition, I'm afraid. It's difficult to hold a scalpel when your fingers tremble." He dropped his gaze to his hands. "Until I am restored and fully healed, my work must match my abilities."

"I should think, with the war effort and all, there might be an advisory position in the military –"

"I've recently returned from Belgium," said Kane, blunt. "I have no intention of ever returning."

Hatch gave a little startle. "Oh! You've seen fighting, then?"

"Some."

"The newspaper claims we got the Huns in a tizzy, what with the recent thrust from Douai over Vimy Ridge," George said, "I've heard folks say, the war'll be done by harvest-time." His smile was the toothy display of an eager child. "Won't that be grand! A Christmas without war, and all the boys, home from the Front! Will it happen, do ya think?"

Kane measured the hope in the man's features. "I doubt it," he replied.

"You ain't the kind of man to sugar-coat, are you," George said.

"My patients didn't come to me for my bedside manner."

George leaned back in the seat. "Our doctor in Okotoks? He's a kindly fella but too sociable and not very precise. You, though…" George smiled. "You seem mightily precise."

Kane cast him a side-long glance.

"I am."

"You take pride in a job well-done?"

"I do."

George studied Kane for a long moment, tapping his foot against the wooden floor of the carriage. "I have a business, and it's a busy one. I could use a spot of help, especially with summer coming," he said. "I wonder if Providence might have put us together on this train, so I could ask you to come work for me while you're getting back your strength."

Kane narrowed his eyes.

"What manner of business?"

George weighed out his reply, as carefully as a butcher measures a rasher of bacon.

"A business of flesh and blood, sir."

Kane let this sink in. How could he refuse such an enigmatic request? He had no expectations nor anyone waiting for him, no destination to call home. Perhaps, as this jolly fellow had observed, fair Providence was stepping in to guide him.

When the train pulled into Calgary an hour later, Kane disembarked after George Hatch, ready and willing to launch a new career.

However, as ready and willing as he thought he might be, Kane was unprepared for Okotoks.

The gravel road led through a pitiful collection of dusty, wind-worn buildings – a square hotel, an automobile repair shop, retails stores and lunch counters.

"Welcome to the Heart of the Oilfields," said George's brother, Frank, a rangy, raw-boned man with small open wounds peppering the left half of his face. He said they were cold sores, but Kane recognized a syphilis rash when he saw it.

"Not a big place," said Kane.

George noted the question hiding in the comment. "We get plenty of business, don't you worry. Most of our work comes from Calgary."

"A man's reputation is everything," said the youngest brother, Lou, who'd been waiting for them at the station. The man's voice brimmed with admiration when he said, "George is an artist."

The buggy hopped over potholes. They veered left out of town and, at a leisurely pace, headed west for almost an hour. In the distance, Kane spotted a gigantic, glacial rock with a crack bisecting it, top to root. It looked like a colossal stone table, smashed by a divine fist, and it was the only item that interrupted the endless grassy foothills.

Kane nodded in its direction. "That's quite the landmark."

"Big Rock? Yeah, sure is! The Blackfoot folks call it 'Okotok', so that's what the town got named. Closest thing you'll find to a cliff, this side of the Rockies." George pointed ahead – they'd travelled far enough that a small fringe of blue mountains appeared tiny and delicate along the horizon. Kane felt the stir of amazement in his chest. He knew, their smallness was only a trick of the light and distance.

When Big Rock was reduced to a small hump behind them, the buggy stopped at a low white house surrounded by endless pasture, and the horse gave a snort to the other horses and dairy cattle, grazing in the fields. Children of various ages swarmed around the barn and the outbuildings. They didn't pay the buggy any mind – they were too engrossed in their game of tag – but two women emerged from the house at the sound of their arrival: a young woman with rich brown hair and deep black eyes, lithe and slim except that she was half-way through her pregnancy. Behind her loomed a formidable matron in a long black dress and white lace shawl. She had a harsh face, comprised of severe features and straight lines.

"It took you long enough, Lou," she replied, "You've been gone most of the day. Were you boys drinking in town again?"

"Of course not, Ma," said Frank.

"The train was late," said George as he dismounted and embraced the woman. She remained stiff and unyielding to his affection.

"How were your cousins in Regina?"

"Fine," he replied.

"Did you manage to get a lead on a better breed of cattle?"

"I met a man who can spare a few bull calves, come spring," George said, "The herd will be back to prime health by this time, next year."

As Kane disembarked, her sharp eyes snapped to him. "Who is this, then?"

"Meet Hector, Ma," said Frank, "He's gonna lend a hand with the business."

"Cockamamie foolishness," she muttered and shuffled inside.

The younger woman rolled her eyes as the old woman disappeared. "Ma Hatch has been peevish all day," she said in a quiet voice. "You're most welcome here, Mr. Hector. I'm Sarah, Lou's wife."

"The mother of all my boys! Ain't she a stunner?" he said as he swept her up in his arms. She fell into a fit of girlish giggles and set a peck on Lou's cheek before following her mother-in-law into the home.

The two women provided a fine dinner. After the men shared a game of cribbage and enjoyed their pipes on the back porch, George called Sarah out of the kitchen and asked her to set Kane up in the bunkhouse. Then he bid Kane good-night, and promised to meet him at dawn to show him the nature of their work.

Sarah took a stack of linens and led Kane out to the bunkhouse, which sat alongside a squat red barn. Inside, he found a private room with an iron stove and a sway-back cot, and a small, greasy window with a view of the foothills.

"Come in, Mr. Hector," she bid in her quiet voice, "I'll make the bed for you and light the fire."

"Please, I can do that myself. I don't wish to be a burden," he said, noting her clumsiness. "How far along are you, if you don't mind me asking?"

"Almost five months," she replied.

"And all is progressing well?" The question hung between them, a sudden awkwardness in the air, and Kane hastily added, "I am a doctor, madame. Or, I was. But there's no need to answer me, if you feel I'm prying."

She let out her breath in a coo. "Oh! A doctor! I'm fine, thank you for asking."

"Tired, I imagine."

Sarah let out a chuckle. "Ma Hatch doesn't allow for laziness."

He took the linens from her as she went outside to gather wood, and as she lit the fire, he attempted to make the bed. His fingers were weak. The sheet slipped in his grasp.

"I can do it," she insisted, and took the sheets from him. "That's my chore. Besides, I can see you are weary after your long journey."

He stepped back, massaging his aching hands as she finished her tasks. Not another word passed between them until he bid her good-night when she left.

The bigger barns housed the cattle and horses, but the squat red barn had quite another purpose. The first hint was a fire pit with an iron cauldron, built nearby in the yard. The next was a stack of wood – some chopped and stacked for burning, but others, hacked and hewn into the rough shape of horse heads. As the sun rose, George waited at the open barn door. He welcomed Kane inside.

Along the far wall was a workbench of heavy lumber, slashed and stained by years of use. There were crates and boxes of supplies, barrels of pickling salt, a shelf carrying a wide range of empty glass jars, and a selection of knives in all sizes, hung from pegs. The smell was earthy and copper-tinged, with the acrid overtones of wood scrubbed with bleach, which reminded Kane of an operating room after surgery. From one iron hook in a stall's cross-beam hung the shoulder hump and head of a gigantic bison; on another, dangled an entire wolverine. The main floor by the workbench was covered in stone tiles and diligently swept, but inside the stalls, the ground was strewn with hay to sop up any fluids. The last stall contained only a gigantic pile of sawdust.

His time in Belgium and his childhood in Montreal caught up with him; Kane whispered, "*Mon dieu!*"

Lou and George were already deep in discussion, leaning against the stall partitions. "These arrived yesterday with the morning post," said Lou. "A big-shot hunter from New York, holidaying down in Montana at the Many Glacier Hotel, heard about your technique from the guides. He had them shipped overnight by stage."

"He saw our grizzly in the main lodge?"

"I suppose he must," said Lou. "He wanted only the best." Lou pointed to the wolverine. "I took out the guts, real careful like you showed me, but I was afraid you weren't gonna get back in time b'fore they spoiled."

George looked invigorated.

"We best hop to it!" he said to Kane, rubbing his hands together. "There's an extra rubber apron behind the doors."

"Just look at the size of that buffalo noggin!" said Lou in admiration. "I didn't think they got so big no more."

"It's going to take all three of us to move it," said George.

It took six, actually. They roped three of the oldest boys into helping as they carefully transferred the bison's head to the tiled floor. George selected a gleaming, curved knife that was as sharp as the north wind.

The woolly brown hide was swiftly loosened with two carefully-considered cuts, then gingerly peeled from the skull like the skin of an orange.

"We got a mount prepared?" said George.

"I whittled one yesterday," Lou said, and when he shoo'd the rambunctious boys back outside, he followed them out and continued towards the wood pile.

"Hector," said George, "On the shelf by the desk, you'll find a jar of pink liquid. Bring it here."

The pickle jar was large; the liquid inside, slimy, soapy, and translucent.

George had already spread the skin of the head across the workbench, fur side down. A few strings of white fat clung to the cheeks, and George used the flat of his blade to scrape this away. Once done, he took the jar from Kane and opened the lid. A fragrance like flowers and soured cabbage belched out.

"What the devil is that?"

"My secret recipe," George replied with a merry wink. He grabbed a pair of hog-bristle brushes from the shelf. "Borax and lavender oil, mostly." He handed a brush to Kane. "Paint it generous-like across the flesh, working out towards the edges. When we start the tanning process, it keeps the skin from turning rancid and retains its pliability."

Such was Kane's first task as a taxidermist-in-training.

Taxidermy was hot, hard, heavy work. It demanded a measure of precision and fastidiousness much like a surgery. Too few cuts, and the skin would pull or tear; too many, and the resulting piece looked like Frankenstein's monster. Workspaces must always be clean, or the fluids of one dead creature would stain the fur of another. The chemicals and solutions had to be dutifully labeled, tidied and put away in alphabetical order, and never allowed to mix. Knives were sharpened after every task; tools were polished until they shone.

George was a patient teacher, but Frank left them whenever there were heavier tasks; he had no interest in gore. He ran the day-to-day of the dairy, and perhaps because of his love for his cows, he had grown to be a sensitive fellow. He couldn't even twist a chicken's neck. But between George, Lou and Kane, they made short work of most animals that arrived in the shop, some from as far away as Idaho or Edmonton. 'Hatch Bros. Taxidermy' enjoyed a fine reputation, and the surprise of it pleased Kane most: opening a crate was like opening a gift. Inside could be a lynx, or a trumpeter swan, as a snake or a sturgeon. The sheer variety of God's creatures humbled him.

Sometimes, in quiet hours, George and Kane amused each other with the bits of animals that had been left behind. They'd lay them out on the workbench and move them like puzzle pieces, and create exciting combinations that no merciful deity would dare. A deer's heart with the legs of a duck, or the tail of a carp bumped against a weasel skull. Or, strangest of all, a cluster of gooey eyeballs surrounded by sparrow wings, with four tiny rubber tires arranged in a square around it. Kane recognized the tires as coming from a dinky toy, many of which could be found scattered in the yard.

"D'you get it?" said George eagerly, as if he was waiting for a punchline. When Kane didn't answer, he replied, "It's an angel!"

Kane furrowed his brow. "What have you been smoking, to think that looks *angelic*?"

"Don't you read your Bible?" George teased. "That's what they look like!"

"By who's description?"

"Ezekiel, that's who!" George replied, "He wrote, 'And their whole body, and their backs, and their hands, and their wings, and the wheels, were full of eyes round about, even the wheels that they four had.'" He started to guffaw.

Kane scoffed. "Make me wonder, what was Ezekiel smoking!?"

George snorted even harder. "You're a good man, Hector," he said once he'd caught his breath, clapping him on the back.

They both admired the collection of animal parts on the workbench.

"I don't want to throw this one away," George said.

"It's much too funny for the dog dish," Kane agreed.

The inspiration came to them simultaneously, as if some greater cosmic force had blessed them both in unison, knowing the work required two dark senses of humour, two sets of eager hands, and two clever intellects. A single man might have the thought and let it go, content to amuse himself with just the concept, but two men? They would build and bounce ideas back and forth, playing the parts of both audience and entertainer, and the idea would naturally expand into something magnificent.

George grabbed an empty pickle jar.

"I'll mix up some brine," said Kane.

They arranged the pieces with creative glee: the four wheels at the bottom, the sparrow wings spread out along the edges, the rest of the jar filled with as many eyeballs as George could scrounge from the rubbish heap.

When the pickling brine was mixed and boiled, Kane delicately ladled it into the jar, unwilling to disturb the arrangement. A few of the smaller eyes bobbed and rolled. The smell was greasy and gamey, a bit like wild pork.

At last, with the hot jar sitting in the centre of the work bench, they admired their pickled angel. George gave a coo of delight. His eyes twinkled.

"We gotta enter this in the exhibition at the Calgary Stampede," he said.

The vision of their terrifying angel, sitting alongside cucumbers and carrots, threw Kane into fits of uncharacteristic mirth so loud and unbridled, his laughter echoed from the roof-beams. In retrospect, he was fairly sure he'd never laughed so hard in all his life.

The angel won first prize.

There could be no greater advertisement for Hatch Bros. Taxidermy than a blue ribbon at the Calgary Stampede. The news wire picked up the story and sent it across the nation. Folks from as far away as Chicago sent letters, looking to purchase their own pickled angel. Even a circus man from out West expressed keen interest, eager to build a travelling show.

Business, which had already been increasing with the arrival of warm weather, suddenly exploded. The men bent their heads to their work and called for a few of the older boys to assist – Sarah and Lou had ten children, all strapping lads, so there was plenty of selection. Kane worked tirelessly at George's elbow, taking many of the small projects on his own. Sometimes his hands still trembled, but dead flesh was more forgiving than live patients, and taxidermy offered the freedom to take his time, consider his actions, and rest when his weak hands required it. His injury prevented him from lifting larger weights, so Kane preferred to work with the whole bodies of vermin or birds, rather than the heads and shoulders of larger game.

"You really bring 'em back to life," said George as he admired a fox in mid-leap.

Predictably, Ma Hatch wasn't impressed. She regarded Kane with mild distrust and never spoke to him about anything more than the basics. The old woman rarely left the house, only going as far as the front porch, from which she complained bitterly when her boys came late to dinner, smelling of vinegar and offal. Her complaints dried up, however, when George bought her a Model T and took her for a drive through Okotoks.

Sarah was more charitable. She didn't understand the appeal of taxidermy, but she was kind enough to pretend. At the root of it, she was too practical for the display of trophies. Her pleasure came from creating items with use: a new knit-sweater with pearl buttons, or a doily for the table, or a delicious apple pie. She worked endlessly, dawn to dusk, to keep the house clean and all the menfolk fed, often scurrying from task to task -- whatever Ma Hatch demanded, Sarah performed. It didn't matter that she had grown as round as a pear. Ma said the work needed to be done, and Sarah had good strong limbs, so she might as well take satisfaction in her duty.

Every noon, Sarah delivered a basket of lunch to the small barn. The meal was always the same hearty fare. Boiled eggs, a soup of salt jerky, brown bread with fresh butter. Delicious, but unsurprising.

George would tease her for her habits. Lou would pretend that his order had been mixed up and demand that the waiter lose his job. "This isn't my beef Wellington!" he'd boom, and the brothers would snicker and chortle. Sarah would smile but say nothing. The same scene played out each afternoon.

Kane never complained.

One night, after a long day of tanning an elk's hide and a hearty dinner of elk stew, Kane withdrew to the back porch of the farm house to enjoy a pipe of fresh tobacco. His hands ached. He'd bought a new tin at the general store, but his pen knife wobbled as he sliced the foil liner open. He fumbled, almost dropped the tin, and found it impossible to pinch the leaves and pack the bowl.

"Might I help?" said a mild voice.

Sarah stood in the kitchen door, wiping her hands on the hem of her apron.

Before that moment, she'd rarely said two words to him. Certainly, she'd never initiated a conversation! His heart beat ferociously in his chest, but he wasn't sure why. Perhaps, he thought, he'd grown too accustomed to the simple company of dead animals. A discussion with a real live woman posed a frightful challenge.

"There's no need. I almost have it."

"A man deserves a smoke, after all the hard work put in during the day," she said, holding out her hands. "You must be mighty tired."

She was willing to give him an excuse for his disability. He took it.

"Quite exhausted," he replied, handing the pipe and tobacco over.

With small measured movements, she tucked a small amount of shredded leaf into the bowl and pressed it down with her graceful thumb, repeating until the bowl was full. Then she handed it back to him, allowing Kane to bend forward as she struck a match. He puffed, then let the fire die. She tamped down the ashes. Suitably prepared, they lit the pipe together once more. As the smooth smoke filled his lungs, his heartbeat returned to its regular rhythm.

"Thank you, Mrs. Hatch," he said.

"My father smoked a pipe," she said, "I've always loved the smell."

"Even now?"

She laid one hand on her belly. "Smoke doesn't bother me. It did, with the earlier pregnancies, but not this one."

"Are you eating enough? Sleeping well?"

"When I can," she replied. "I've only got a month left. I'll be relieved when it's over." Then she lowered her gaze to his hands. "I hope you don't mind my prying, but... do they bother you much?"

"They ache."

"I have a recipe for a cream to soften hard skin," she said, "My sisters used to make it for my pop; he had tough callouses from working the fields. When I saw your scars, I thought –" She stopped, fearing she'd trespassed.

He turned over one hand. The sleeve was rolled up, and the line slashed across his wrist looked puckered and red in the evening light. "I'd appreciate if you make some," he replied.

They watched the shadows lengthen over the pasture as he enjoyed the pipe, and she seemed to relish the scent of smoke dancing on the hot summer air. He thought how sweet a life could be here in Okotoks. Save a little money, maybe open a practice and serve as the town doctor when the current one retires. Perhaps marry a young lady and start a family. It was a pleasing and novel diversion, for him to consider setting down roots.

"You say you have sisters?" he said, one eyebrow arched.

"Six," she replied.

But the comforting dream of home and family vanished when the harsh tone of Ma Hatch erupted from the kitchen. "Where's that girl? Sarah! Sarah!? The stew pot isn't scrubbed yet! What are you doing, loitering?"

Sarah closed her eyes to muster strength.

"Thank you again," said Kane, holding up the pipe.

She nodded and retreated inside to finish her tasks.

The next day, when Sarah brought lunch to the small barn, the basket held sandwiches of sliced chicken and bacon, with tart apples and ginger cookies for dessert. Lou was delighted.

"Did the waiter get your order right, honey?" she teased as she handed out the sandwiches, each one wrapped neatly in wax paper.

"It's not beef Wellington, but I'm too hungry to complain!" he said and kissed her cheek. George dove into his meal with gusto. Kane, however, experienced a strange sense of foreboding with the change in routine – almost like remembering a long-forgotten poem. Weeks of boiled eggs, and now this? It sparked confusion.

But the sandwiches were delicious, and the cookies were sublime, so he dared not bring it up. He didn't want this unease to be misconstrued as ungratefulness.

"What are you working on today?" she asked as they ate, glancing around the barn at the bits of animals in various states of preservation.

Lou laughed. "What do you care?"

"I'm curious!"

"Ma Hatch will burn that curiosity right out of you, if she sees," said Frank, "A woman's place is in the home."

Sarah leaned against the workbench, suddenly winded.

None of the men seemed to notice, so Kane grabbed a wooden stool from the end of the workbench and set it next to her. He helped her sit down. Her ankles were swollen. At a glance, he noted her hands were, too.

"Look at that, a little chivalry," Frank teased, and said to George, "Sir Hector is making us look bad."

But Kane did not rise to the comment. He'd noticed a grey cast to her face.

"Are you well?"

She waved off the comment.

He would not be dissuaded.

"You have another month yet, correct?"

The men, who had been wolfing down their sandwiches, paused at such a personal comment. Lou, in particular, seemed offended.

"You keeping track of my wife's condition?"

"Someone must, you oaf," he replied. "You aren't?"

Lou sniffed at that, but George laughed. "You ain't a doctor here, Hector."

"Once a doctor, *always* a doctor," he scoffed. "Medicine is my true vocation."

"*Ooh la la*, ain't you Mister High-And-Mighty," Frank chortled, but Lou had grown stern, and for the first time, seemed to notice his wife's declining condition.

"Is she okay?"

Sarah struggled to breathe easily. Kane crouched before her, holding her hands, which were cracked and dry from chores.

"Is the baby moving?"

"Yes, but," she said between gasps. "Too early for labor."

"Let us not concern ourselves with that yet," he said, calm and low.

"My back... aching fierce... all day," she said.

"Did the pains come on quickly?"

She nodded. "When I was scrubbing the floors."

"And what about the baby?" he said, laying one palm on her arm and the other on the swell of her stomach. Lou stood up and clenched fists at such an act of intimacy, but Kane ignored the man and kept his attention on Sarah. "Has the baby turned?"

She nodded. "I think so." Her breath quivered.

He swore under his breath.

"Frank, you and Lou help Sarah to the house to lie down," said Kane, "George, I need you to head to town and fetch the midwives, as fast as the Model T will take you."

Sarah let out a mewl. Sweat broke across her forehead. Her eyes were full of fear, but Kane helped her to her feet and, with Lou and Frank under each arm, they slowly returned to the main house.

Ma Hatch scolded Sarah for working too hard, but they ignored the old woman and climbed the stairs to the bedrooms. Kane turned down the bed. The men helped the struggling mother, easing her down onto the mattress, plumping pillows around her. Kane instructed Lou to get cool clothes, and for Frank to boil water, and for Sarah to raise her feet on yet more pillows. He encouraged her to breathe steadily, slowly. For a long time, he sat on the side of her bed and held her hand, breathing in synchronicity.

After a quarter of an hour, the pace of her exhalations relaxed.

"I've gone and made a fuss," she said in shame.

"Never mind," he replied. "You took a turn."

"It's too early for the baby."

"Surely, after squeezing out ten of the little monsters, you must know that babies keep their own schedule," he replied, trying to impart a little levity. "I'm more concerned for you."

Her fingers squeezed his.

"You've felt strange all day, haven't you."

She nodded.

"I thought it odd that you'd change your routine," he replied.

"You could tell the baby had turned from my sandwiches?" She gave a wheeze of astonishment. "I only wished to be kind!"

"You're feeling maternal," he corrected. "We are all slaves to our physical form. A flush of blood to the brain, or to the heart, or to the liver – these are our bodies' chemical reactions to our environment. They'll change our routines and make us do things that our rational minds normally wouldn't consider. Our flesh can turn our thoughts against us."

She looked to his hands, to the narrow wrists, and she turned them over to display the thick, ropy scars.

"Was this a mere reaction to your body's changing chemistry?"

"Yes," he said. "A flush of chemicals, released by fear."

"Fear?"

He nodded. "Fear of loss is the most powerful reaction of all."

She pressed her lips together.

"What did you lose, Dr. Kane?"

It was a question he had not taken time to ponder, but she waited for his answer with saint-like patience. He thought of the hell of Belgium in the final days before his attempt, when the screams of dying men haunted every minute of the day, and there was no respite from gunfire or explosions, and his fingers never stopped trembling. The entire world was constructed from mud, bones, and death. As the sounds of battle rang in his ears, he feared that he'd never feel a moment's peace again.

At last, he said, "I lost all hope."

The remainder of the afternoon was spent on tenterhooks. The men returned to the small barn and their work. The army of boys saw to the tasks of the farm. Ma Hatch resumed her regular badgering, except that there was no one to finish the chores, and Sarah was reminded at every turn of her laziness.

By mid-afternoon, George returned from Okotoks – Madge in the General Store said the midwives were busy up at the old Chesterman farm, so instead, he'd brought the town physician. Dr. Ernest was a rotund man of short stature and red nose with a forked red beard and speckled hands. He blustered around the house and grounds, spending a few minutes examining the patient, tapping on the soles of her feet with his index finger and pressing his hairy ear to her belly. Then he spent an hour on the porch, enjoying lemonade and cookies while flirting with Ma Hatch.

Dr. Ernest proclaimed Sarah to be in fine health, as long as she stayed off her feet. The baby was strong and would make it to full term. Lou was ecstatic. After paying the doctor's bill, he thanked Kane for such quick thinking and for noticing what he had not. He promised to be a more attentive husband and father in future.

Kane was exhausted in a way he'd not felt since his stint in the war. He was as wrung out as an old rag. After dinner, George suggested the men go to town for a celebratory drink with Ernest, but Kane declined. Instead, he fell into his cot in the bunkhouse and allowed himself to sleep.

But in the darkest hour of night, a faint knock came upon the bunkhouse door.

The sound woke Kane slowly. At first, he thought it might be the figment of a dream, but then he heard the scrape and sob, and knew the sounds were real. He pulled on his trousers and undershirt, then fumbled to light the oil lamp, his thin fingers shaking.

Sarah sat at the threshold, curled in the dirt. Blood stained her night gown. She clutched a bundled sweater to her breasts, and the pearl buttons looked like children's teeth in the amber lamplight. She lifted large, black, horrified eyes to him.

Kane immediately suppressed a surge of terror.

"I couldn't find the chamber pot," she whimpered, "Ma Hatch took it to clean but she didn't bring it back."

"You walked to the outhouse?" he admonished. "You were to stay in bed!"

"Fresh air," she said. She spoke in desperate sentence fragments. "Lou, still gone." She struggled to her naked feet and limped inside, spattering a trail of blood in her wake.

"Damn," he said, more to himself than her, but she started to sob.

"She came," Sarah sobbed, "In the outhouse, she came."

The sweater was soaked with blood. In the centre lay the pale pink form, curled as if sleeping. Kane thought of a newly-hatched bird in a nest. Closed eyes, lids as dusky as iris petals. Tiny hands like giblets. Sarah held the sweater up to him like an offering.

"Oh, God," he whispered.

"A girl," Sarah continued, "Finally, a girl."

There was no life in the little face, only emptiness. Yet Sarah admired it, smiled at it, and wept tears that might have been joy. She pressed her gift towards Kane.

"Please," she said, "I can't lose her."

"Mrs. Hatch," he said, then more gently, "Sarah, you must lie down or you'll hemorrhage." He flailed about for a direction. He was a doctor, not a midwife! Panic threatened again but he pushed it away. "Come, let me help you," he said, keeping his voice steady, just like he had with the men, mortally wounded in the trenches. "Over to the cot. That's a good girl." He eased her down on the thin mattress. As she reclined, the blood seeped more slowly, and she passed her placenta without notice. It slid into the blankets, slack and crimson; one half was smooth, like a slab of liver, while the other was torn and ragged, covered in knobby black clots. The bloodless white umbilical cord connected it to the tiny form still cradled in her protective arms.

"They'll take her from me," Sarah continued. The bright tang of desperate madness crept into the corners of her words. "They'll take her away, Hector, and I'll never see her again."

"Hush," he said as he cut the cord with his pen-knife.

"I can't bear to lose her," Sarah continued. "I've been trying so long. So long! A girl, Hector!" She clung to him. "I only ever wanted a girl."

"Sarah…" he said, his head still bent to the task of examining the woman. To his relief, the blood had stopped flowing from between her thighs.

"If they take her, they'll bury her in the cold earth, and I don't know what I'll do," she rasped, but the anguish in her voice told him clearly, she knew exactly what path she'd choose. Pain flared through his scars at the memory.

Kane spoke in carefully measured words.

"She's gone, Sarah," he said, as kindly as he could.

But Sarah's eyes remained brittle and vivid.

"Please, Hector," she begged. "Don't let them take my little Hope."

Never had a word struck so powerful a blow.

Like a parasite, the madness crept out of her and into him. Tranquility washed over her tired features as a frantic need infested him, swelled in his guts, turned his reason into manic action. Obsession grasped him tightly and refused to let go. He took the delicate bundle from Sarah's arms and left her to sleep in the bunk house while he scurried to the small barn. He set the sweater and its gruesome contents upon the workbench, placing his oil lamp to one side so that the light would illuminate the table.

A glass jar from the shelf.

The pink liquid, Borax and lavender.

A brine of salt.

He worked like a man possessed, never once considering the consequences of his actions. He knew, too keenly, the overwhelming grief of the woman resting in the bunk house, and he was afraid that she'd do something drastic if she was denied.

As the sun rose, he heard the first cries of worry coming from the main house. Lou must've discovered that Sarah was not in their marriage bed.

Yet still, he wasn't done.

He worked as the sounds of people percolated from outside, searching the farm with growing desperation, and he heard the great hue rise up when George located Sarah in the bunkhouse, sleeping deeply after the loss of so much blood. Still, he continued. It wasn't until Lou opened the doors of the small barn that Kane paused to wipe sweat from his brow. He let out a long, tired breath.

"I'm done."

Lou looked at the jar on the table.

Horror spread across his features. He could not speak; he only gave a pained yelp like a wounded animal.

"Sarah could not bear to lose the baby," Kane explained. "She asked me –"

But the morning quiet shattered as Lou released a blood-curdling scream, pitched high and intense. Alerted by the sound, George dashed from the direction of the bunkhouse, with Frank and the boys close behind him. They were drawn to the sound like a swarm of hornets.

George, the fastest, skidded to a stop on the threshold.

"How could you?!" Lou screamed, "How?! God have mercy, how?!"

The other boys were almost there – brothers and sons. George stared at Hector for one horrified moment, then his senses returned to him, and before the curious children could peep inside the barn, he turned and instructed them to fetch Ma Hatch, then to run to town and get Doctor Ernest.

Lou screamed again, this time in clear words.

"Bring the sheriff!"

"But Sarah asked me," pleaded Kane. "She'll tell you herself. She begged me! She said she couldn't lose her precious little girl. I thought, if only I could do this for her, she might be able to bear the loss of the child."

Lou collapsed to the ground, his hands entangled in his hair, his head bent over until his brow touched the earth. He screamed and screamed like the revolution of a wheel on dry bearings.

"Ask her, George!" said Kane. "Ask her and she'll tell you!"

George came no closer.

His expression was a strange compromise between pity, agony, and regret. His voice rasped.

"She's dead, Hector."

Reason and sense came rushing in. "I thought... when I left her...." Kane felt his hands quake, his blood chill. "She was alive when I left, only sleeping!" His eyes flashed to the jar, to the evidence of his misguided compassion, which none could understand save for the woman now growing cold and stiff where he'd left her.

Through the open barn door, he caught sight of the eldest boy racing off in the Model T, bouncing over the gravel road towards the Big Rock and the town of Okotoks. The doctor and the law would arrive within the hour.

"But George, I didn't –"

"Don't try to explain, Hector," said George. "You'll only make it worse."

"I didn't kill her!"

"I know, friend, but that don't matter," George replied. "Not with that on the table, and her in your bed." The man stepped to the side of the doors, giving Kane an avenue of escape. The distant fringe of the blue Rocky Mountains lay hazy and bold in the distance, and George's unspoken message was clear. Freedom lay to the west, if only Kane was quick enough.

Kane glanced one last time to his most-perfect work, carefully preserved and meticulously crafted. The angelic face, soft as if sleeping. The half-moon of dark eyelashes. The tiny hands, clasped in prayer. For years to come, he would dream of that innocent face, and whenever he smelled lavender, he thought of her.

Eventually, his collection of pickled punks would rival the greatest anatomical museums of Europe. He would join a travelling show, and people would come from miles around to admire his creations, and just the name of Dr. Hector Kane would sell fistfuls of tickets. However, none of his creations would ever soothe his guilt. No amount of admiration or wonder could quell his grief. He'd struggle and strive to capture the verisimilitude of life in every subsequent piece, but it didn't matter, because regardless of how many wondrous creatures he devised, Hector Kane would forever see himself as a failure.

Kane had only wished to restore Hope, but all hope was gone.

The Merrow

Cecil's first memory was of water: inky swells of seawater reflecting silver crescents of moonlight, calling out to him like a mother holding out her arms. He must have been three years old, for in this recollection, he is standing on the edge of a dock where his father has tied up their trawler, *The Merrow*, and by all accounts, that particular vessel sideswiped the rocks at Discovery Passage when he was only four, after which her hull busted open like a ripe peach and she ingloriously sank.

In this memory, as a toddler standing on the wharf near the fishing boat, he remembers his father's back is turned, for the man is busy loading supplies onto the fishing boat with a million thoughts occupying every wrinkle and curve of his brain. Seagulls wheel and cry overhead. The air smells of salt and creosote, and bits of punky driftwood afloat under the pilings. Cecil remembers gazing out over the water and hearing a soft melody in the air. In that singular moment, Cecil recalled thinking that an easy step off the edge of the dock would take him directly home.

The water was cold but he liked it. The blackness swallowed him up; the current sucked him down. Bubbles surrounded him on all sides -- suspended silver orbs in the endless dark -- and they twirled as he drifted amongst them. In hindsight, he knew that they must've been moon jellies caught in the rising tide, for bubbles would have ascended towards the surface, not spun in place.

Even with his ears full of rushing water, the melody remained. He heard the soft lilt of mysterious words and he yearned to follow the song, but he had not yet learned to swim and so had no way to propel himself through the murk and the gloom. Maybe, he thought as a child, he could spurt out a jet of air -- just a wee fart! -- and push himself along like an octopus.

But the air came out, not in a jet, but in a puff, and transformed into a pulsing ribbon of useless bubbles -- more whimsical and dynamic than the jellies -- so that the fart accomplished nothing except reduce his buoyancy and sink him down.

Then came a thunderous swish, a pale hand, a fracturing of the perfectly placid and peaceful darkness: Cecil remembered himself being snatched by the collar from the sanctuary of the sea and hauled upwards like a basket of herring. Upon breaking the surface, the watery silence was replaced with piercing cries for help and the quick noisy rhythm of feet running across the dock planks. He was laid out flat on the slimy boards so that strong palms could push the liquid from his lungs, but all the hustle was unnecessary. The boy was fine. He burped up what little water was left in his esophagus with a guttural sputtering cough, no worse for wear.

"Bless your mother's heart," said his father before crushing him in a bear hug.

When he asked, many years later, why his father had said such a strange thing, his father explained that he'd been under the water for too long, and what seemed like only seconds to Cecil had been minutes to the rest. The men heard the splash and searched the dark salt-chuck under the docks but, as heartbeats ticked by without sight of him, they'd assumed the child had drowned.

"O'course, I should've known better, lad," said his father.

"Why?"

"Because of your mother," came the blunt reply. "Bless her heart."

Cecil had no recollection of his mother and this was all the fisherman ever said about the matter. Further questions met with stony silence.

Years passed. A fisherman's life was unforgiving and, much to Cecil's dismay, his father grew wizened and crooked before his time. The old man sold the boats and the fishing equipment and, with a bit of prodding from Cecil, moved into a seaside convalescent home in Esquimalt, where he could live out the last of his days in comfort. He could be quite peevish if he spent too much time indoors. However, when he spent an afternoon sitting on a deck chair, gazing out across the sun-dappled bay to watch the waves dance, it put him in a loquacious mood. Advanced age made the man's mind wander while loosening his tongue. He was no longer so tight-lipped as he had been when his mind was young and sharp.

One fine spring day, sitting alongside his father on the porch of the home, Cecil asked, "All these years and you've never told me, but I wish to know: who was my mother?"

"A pretty face," came the cryptic reply.

This new tidbit of information piqued his interest. The young man took the opportunity presented him.

"Did she love to swim?"

"Oh, aye, she did!" This was said with a frill of jolly laughter. "She was a lovely bit of fluff. Very tall and thin, much like you. You have your mother's eyes, too, and a bit of her in your smile."

"Where did you meet her?"

"On the rocks by Clallam Bay," he said, "Her family lives there."

Cecil felt a jolt of surprise ricochet through him like an electrical current. "I have family in Washington State? Just across the Strait of Juan de Fuca?" he said in awe, for it had always been just his father and him, a couple of lonely bachelors, and the idea that he might have blood relatives was intoxicating. "Do I have cousins? Or aunts and uncles?"

His father's mood took a sudden turn. "Don't get it in your head to look for 'em," he commanded. "They will not take you in. Don't even try."

"Why?"

"They are not so fond of me," he replied. "And with you? Ho ho, they'll be doubly mad that you even exist!" This seemed to cause the old man a great deal of wicked joy -- he chortled and snorted so loudly, the petite nurse named Emily-Ann left her desk to look out the door and make sure the old man wasn't choking. He waved away her concerns. At last, he calmed down enough to continue. "No, I made a promise to your mother to keep you safe and secret from all her kin, and I aim to keep it that way. You must never go looking for your mother's relatives; they're mean and sly and blood-thirsty." He waggled his finger. "They are not fair folk, my lad, no matter what the legends claim."

This made Cecil's eyebrows arch.

"Legends."

"That's what I said," said his father. "Long minutes you were trapped under that dock in the salt-chuck, my lad, and everyone said I'd be pulling up a corpse, but when I grabbed your collar and hauled you out of the ocean and saw your lively eyes with not a spark of fear in them, I knew then that you took after your mother." He leaned in close and dropped his voice to a conspiratorial whisper. "Your mother was a mermaid, my lad, and you're a child of the sea."

Cecil blinked twice.

"Are you feeling alright, Dad?"

"Never better," came his father's reply.

"Should I call the nurse?"

"Why? Oh, because I said your mother was a mermaid? That's hardly a reason to fetch a nurse. What's a nurse gonna do about it?" His father snorted. "You know it's true. I've seen you on the boats, listening to the splashing of the waves... you can hear the music in it, I wager."

Cecil was not about to feed his father's delusions, so he did not affirm this.

"Plus, you got the webbing between your toes. You try to hide it but I've seen it."

"Many people have webbed toes."

"True, but you can hold your breath a ruddy long time," his father added. "How long, hey? Nine minutes or so, if I remember right. Long enough to swim under the boat to free up the propeller, deep enough to shift the anchor when its caught on a bit of stone! And you swim fast enough to catch us an eel for our dinner! Oh, I remember. You think

I've forgotten all those nights on the boat when we ate well from your catch."

"You raised me on a boat," Cecil replied. "Of course, I know how to swim and catch a fish. I hardly ever stepped on land for the first ten years of life!"

His father nodded. "And it was a good life, too!" His expression softened with nostalgia and longing. "Where is *The Merrow* these days?"

"Up by Discovery Passage," Cecil replied. He dared not mention the sinking of the trawler; the memory would upset the old man.

"Ah, yes, that's where she belongs, my bouncy bonnie little *Merrow*," came the rambling reply. "A bit of eel. That would make a good lunch. I used to eat eel pie -- do you think they have eel pie here? No, I suppose not. On Tuesdays we have tomato soup for lunch."

And thus, the conversation steered itself away from mermaids and lost ships, and Cecil was grateful for it. The world had enough strangeness in it lately: the British freighter *Alum Chine*, carrying a cargo of 343 tons of dynamite, had recently exploded in Baltimore Harbour, and an accident like that puts every sailor and dockworker on edge, no matter where they are. There were grumbles of unrest in Europe, too, and speculation that soon the Dominion of Canada might be at war, joining the British Empire in fighting the Hun. No, Cecil had no appetite for chatter about fairy tales with a senile old man, not when the grim realities of modern life demanded all of his attention.

However, when he left the convalescent home, he mentioned to Nurse Emily-Ann that his father had been acting strange. "Isn't he always," she muttered, sounding tired, but she still made a note of it.

Then Cecil returned to the docks and picked up where he left off, hauling cargo as a longshoreman, living in a boarding house run by a warm-hearted matron, getting up every dawn to work hard and scrape by and be glad for it.

But three months later, an errand boy found him at the docks and pressed a note from the convalescent home into his hand.

Cecil left work immediately and without an explanation to his boss -- even though he knew he'd be fired for it -- and ran as fast as his long, lanky legs would take him, across the peninsula to the south beach, up the wooden steps, passed the empty deck chairs and through the dining hall. Emily-Ann was sitting at her desk but she stood quickly when she saw him enter.

"You must go in right away," she said, ushering him upstairs. "Just after lunch, your father took a turn."

Cecil heard the old man moaning long before they reached the door to his room.

"He was fine yesterday!"

"It can happen quickly with these old dears," she explained.

Cecil wondered if anyone had ever before referred to his father, a grouchy barnacle as salt-weathered as a lighthouse door, as an *'old dear'*.

The nurses had laid out the man as straight as a pike on his bed, staring at the ceiling. Even when Cecil dragged a chair close, sat down, and enveloped his father's calloused hand in both his own, the old man never blinked nor glanced at him. He let out a litany of painful creaking groans, like the prow of a wooden ship hammered by a storm's assault.

"I'm here now, Dad," Cecil said, his heart hammering in his chest, the first cold rivulets of dread trickling through his veins. It had always been the two of them. He could scarcely imagine a life without his father, so he snapped shut that line of thought and turned his back to it, terrified of what was to come. Instead, he narrowed his gaze to study his father's features and refused to acknowledge the pallor of Death.

Drool glistened on the chapped lips. The groaning stopped. The dull eyes widened as they fixed upon Cecil's worried face. When the old man spoke, the words were slurred and smeared together. "Your mother came to visit me," he said. "She's promised to take me home with her."

Under his fingers, Cecil barely felt his father's pulse. It felt as faint as the beating of a sculpin's fin.

"Dad, the doctor is on his way."

"Send him back. I'm going home with your mother," came the reply.

He glanced to Emily-Ann. She looked strained. She beckoned, and he joined her in the hall to confer.

"Is your mother coming?" she asked, unsure of this development.

Cecil shook his head. "If I have a mother, I've never met her. It's only been me and Dad, all my life."

"Do you have family to help you?"

"None."

Emily-Ann patted his arm. "You may stay with him as long as you wish," she said, "But I fear he's had a stroke and it's only a matter of time."

With her invitation, Cecil settled into the chair and waited, curling his legs under him and crossing his arms over his chest. The doctor arrived and proclaimed there was nothing to be done, so he left without adding or subtracting anything to the afternoon, and eventually the old man fell into a fitful sleep. He struggled to breathe and he coughed often, until he woke into a hallucinatory state and began mumbling to himself about *The Merrow's* arrival on the midnight tide. Through the open window, Cecil watched evening come in beautiful shades of pink, orange and mauve. The first stars winked to life in the sky. His father's muttering ceased. Soon after, Emily-Ann brought a blanket and a bowl of tomato soup for Cecil, and he thanked her for her kindness but he had no appetite.

His father never said another word. The old man lay on the bed, uncomfortably straight, staring wide-eyed at the ceiling like a drowning man stares at the surface of the sea.

Long after sunset, Cecil startled awake in the chair. The room was dark. The dishes were gone; Emily-Ann must have fetched them. He snorted and rubbed his hands over his face. Sometimes he inhaled so shallowly while sleeping that he went for a while without taking a breath; when that happened, it took Cecil a few moments to get his bearings and remember to fill his lungs. He cast his eyes around the room.

His father's bed lay empty, the sheets cast back.

Grief snatched him by the collar and hauled him boldly into wakefulness. He bolted upright and hurried into the hall, where the lanterns had been turned down low. The house was very still.

"Nurse," he half-whispered, sorrow cracking in his throat. "Nurse!"

Emily-Ann's little silhouette appeared in the stairway.

"Yes?"

"Is he -- Is my father --?"

Cecil began to sob.

She hurried to him and hugged him. "What is it?"

Her confusion only served to confuse him.

"Why didn't you wake me when you came to collect his body?"

Emily-Ann shook her head. "What do you mean?"

"The bed is empty!"

They hurried together to the old man's room. At the sight of the rumpled sheets and vacant pillow, the nurse gave a strangled cry. She left Cecil there to fetch help from her fellows.

He stood for a few moments in shock, and by the time Cecil returned down the stairs to the main lobby, the convalescent home had been plunged into chaos, with nurses and attendants scurrying from room to room, floor to floor, seeking the old man and calling out his name. Emily-Ann noticed Cecil lingering by the main door. She paused before him, her face waxy. "He can't have gone far," she assured him, trying without success to sound calm and collected, "With his condition... he must be here somewhere! We'll find him, sir, I promise." Then she rushed away in a flap.

Cecil retired to the porch.

The swollen moon was rising in the clear eastern sky. The vibrant colours of the sunset had drained away into blues and blacks, and the town had fallen still. Stretching away in either direction, the ragged coastline was peaceful, and the tide had risen just a little, enough to cover the sandbars and beaches.

Far out in the shimmering water, a movement caught his attention.

Two figures stood in the shallows of the mud flats: one he had never seen before, but one he knew as well as his own reflection. His father raised one hand to him in a crisp wave. Cecil, as if in a dream, waved back.

The woman, tall and willowy, sloe-eyed and raven-haired, cupped her hands around her lips. She sang a melody and he instantly recognized the soft distant notes as the song below the waves. He recalled the cold touch of the dark water, the soft velvety caress of the moon jellies suspended around him, and the silent sanctuary of the ocean. Then the woman smiled to him and he saw his own features echoed in hers. She blew him a kiss, grabbed his father's hand, and with a splash of silver water, they vanished.

Cecil watched the ocean waves erase the concentric ripples of their passage. How long he stood on the porch, watching those ripples fade and those waves curl, he did not know, but the wind blew brisk against the tears on his cheeks and the moonlight shone bright on his quivering chin. His father was gone and he was alone, yet he carried no grief in his heart. His tears were not those of sorrow but of gratitude and joy. For the first time in his life, Cecil felt his mother's love.

The Fate of the Alpha

A miserable wind slapped, pummelled and bit at the doctor as he climbed from the deck of the *SS Joan* onto the bobbing rowboat. He settled his tall frame in the stern, folded lean legs along the wind break of wooden crates and jute bundles, and when he nodded that yes, he was as comfortable as circumstances allowed, the helmsman gave a sharp bark. Sailors pressed into their oars, the bow creaked. The first splash of spray glittered from the tips of the paddles. They deepened their stroke and slowly, deliberately, the dory began to slide from underneath the protection of the steam ship, toward the shores of northern Vancouver Island.

Or, as the sailors called it, New Siberia. The nickname, the doctor reflected, was apt: even now, in the earliest days of March, thick drifts of snow mantled the ground where impenetrable conifers met crooked rocky beaches. This was a forest where wolves hunted and bears roamed, a location ripped from the pages of the Brothers Grimm. It was to be his home for the next ten years.

Another gust of wind tore at his scarf and kicked up a spattering of salt water, dampening his face. Of all Queen Victoria's vast and varied colonies, Vancouver Island was nastiest, and most brutish, and as far from the comforts of London as the devil might devise, but a job offer had enticed him, and a scandal involving a married woman and an impending child had sealed his decision. Henry Wright had no great adventurous spirit, and his exile to the West filled him with resigned despair. He was no coal miner, no lumberjack, no man of the earth. The skin of his hands was soft, save for the thickened pad where his finger pressed a scalpel. Bitterness swelled in his throat and he glared again at the wild shore, then looked back at the low decks of the *SS Joan*, which made this run once a fortnight, and which had delivered him to this wild Hell.

A dangerous place, it was, and poorly suited to an English doctor from a noble family.

Last night, over tiny cups of searing vodka, the captain of the *Joan*, a portly Prussian named Alexi Pushkova, had regaled Wright with the tale of the screw-steamer *Alpha*. Pushkova was an ugly, salt-encrusted man with stiff features and hard jaw, but his eyes had grown misty when he spoke of the *S.S. Alpha*. In the ecclesiastical light cast by the coal-oil lamp, the galley had become an intimate confessional. Pushkova lowered his voice with awe at the *Alpha*'s fate. Or maybe, thought Wright, it was a reverence for the weather, a respect for the power of the sea. Maybe the fate of the *Alpha* struck too close to Pushkova's heart: the iron steam ship had been the pinnacle of modern technology, much stronger than Pushkova's beloved wooden *Joan*.

Late on a Saturday evening, two months previous and in inclement weather much like this, the *Alpha* had made its course through Baynes Sound from Victoria, bound for the Colliery wharves south of New Siberia. The flying rain and heavy spray obscured the vision of the pilot, and she was cast up hard on a reef. A young sailor had tossed out a line to secure the damaged vessel, and as the crashing tides pulled back to reveal fifty yards of bare stone, he leapt from the deck to make a desperate dash for shore. In its rhythm, the wave returned, throwing the young man up against the merciless crags. The crew watched with bated breath, eyes straining in the darkness for any hint of life, expecting none. But a shout rose, and they saw him, ragged and wretched but alive. Only the Hand of Providence had saved him, guiding his helpless form into a crevice from whence he climbed, miraculously unscathed.

"So seeing this, de first mate," Pushkova had said, a gleam in his watery eyes, "A mister Wilkenson, good man, he got a line out to secure with the first, and he made so that he could climb down the ropes and run for shore, in between the waves, like. But none on that ship, not crew nor passenger, would dare it, not after seeing the waves swallow up the first man, even if he had lived. So Wilkenson, he starts to threaten, he starts to tell 'em all they are gonna find themselves in the mouth of Hell, if they don't muster up their courage and try to make for shore. Already, the boards are squealing, starting to crack, and the sea water gushing in.

"No, no, no, they are all saying," Pushkova continued, shaking his head with vehemence, "None are going to go. Captain York, the owner of the vessel, he says the *Alpha* is as sound and safe as ever she was, and Mr. Barber, a passenger, he decides it better to wait amongst the rigging for morning light, for a lower tide, for a rescue vessel to find them. De others are starting to agree. So Wilkenson, bloody bastard, he grabs one of de stowaways and tosses him overboard, and the man, screaming and crying like an albatross, hits the ground with both skinny legs pumping, and he don't pay no heed to the waves, in out in out, and one of those mighty swells comes up and whisks him away."

But even this didn't deter Wilkenson who, as the others screamed out in horror, pushed a second stowaway over the side. This man, spurred on by the fate of his comrade, made a mad sprint for the shore and reached it safely. His success was a spur to the rest. The waves tore at the bow, and bits of cargo were floating in the surf -- wooden crates of preserved salmon, sodden papers, the gossamer sheen of coal dust on the water. Every wave shook the steamer like a rat in a terrier's jaws, and daylight, along with any hope of a rescue, was hours away. With Wilkenson shouting threats and brandishing his fists, twenty-seven passengers and crew made the dangerous attempt, until they stood at last on the forested shore.

They huddled together, and with each crash came the howl of physical agony in the darkness, of drowning men with crushed limbs fighting against the storm. At one in the morning, a great rending of timber signalled the *Alpha*'s demise, and the survivors could no longer detect the sounds of human suffering between the roaring waves. The wretches plucked their way along the rocks towards the beacon of a lighthouse in the distance, where the light keeper used his meagre supplies to make them comfortable until morning arrived.

"Dat Wilkenson," Pushkova had whispered, as if Wilkenson was somewhere on the *Joan*, "He mean old son of a bitch, but he good man. He do exactly with stowaways what any captain supposed to do, 'cept happened to save one, dis time." And he let out a bellowing laugh, then a belch that smelt of vodka and pickled herring.

Suddenly the bow of the skiff scraped, wood on pebbles, and the doctor was jerked from his thoughts, thrust back into the present moment. The front oarsmen jumped out and dragged the boat high, and as he rose from his seat, Wright rearranged his scarf to protect his throat from the chill of New Siberia. He leapt to shore with neither the skill nor the grace of the sailors, and caught his heel on a twist of fractured wood, cast up by the waves.

It was a piece of a polished plank, not driftwood. For a moment, his eyes lingered on its smooth surface. It looked like the decking of a ship, well-oiled, and torn from its place by a feral sea.

Ten years, Wright thought again, and his heart stuttered. Ten long years of service in this place, where air and water possess the brute strength to destroy the modern accomplishments of man. He looked up the beach, to where a small wagon with two chestnut ponies waited to take him to the Colliery Office. Ten years of servitude in this godless wilderness, where the snows last until April and the only egress is by sea, on a rickety contraption called the *SS Joan*.

Wright kicked the plank aside and set his jaw, and strode towards the wagon with determination. It was complacency, and waiting for rescue, that had destroyed the last people to linger on the *Alpha*; those who acted to save themselves had been the only souls to survive. He raised his hand to wave to the wagon driver, and with that simple gesture, the doctor embraced his uncertain future. The fate of the *Alpha* had been a tragedy, but in that moment, Henry Wright made a decision: whatever came next, he must rely solely on himself if he wanted to thrive.

The *Alpha*'s fate would not be his own.

Acknowledgments

Thank you thank you! I want to heap plentiful appreciation on the following people who helped bring this anthology to life:

For providing inspiring conversations and answers to weird and obscure questions, many thanks to Gwyneth Cathyl-Huhn, Dawn Copeman, Gwyn Sproule, Sandy McKinnon, Nick Ward, Avigdor Schulman, Melissa Roeske, and Julie Sabey. Thank you, too, to Daryl C. McClary, Fred Poyner IV, Clay Eals, Bob Bartlett, Ralph Hale, Bart van den Berk and LD Cross for their books and articles regarding the *SS Clallam*, the *Karluk* and Leechtown.

For inadvertently kicking off this anthology, thank you to Jamie Bryant, Ellian Bell, Marc Gerrard, and all the CVOX listeners.

For reading and providing valuable feedback, thank you to Cindy Bannerman, Kailli Pigott, Zach Johnston, Dez Johnston, Kate Blood, Ellie Pigott, Craig Pigott, Jonathan Pigott, Tracy Jenneson, Jennye Holm, and Jeff Holm.

For oodles of support and encouragement, both in reaching new readers and digging into historical oddities, thank you to Rosslyn Shipp, Kera McHugh, Evelyn Gillespie, Meaghan Cursons, Danette Boucher, Kim Letson, Crystal Cahill from @books_in the wild, Clinton Nellist, Patty Marriott, the Goddesses of the Book, and Sisters in Crime. Thank you to everyone who has asked me for a novel that is suitable for young adult readers, too. I hope this helps fill the gap.

Thank you to the folks at *The Montreal Review* for originally publishing 'The Fate of the Alpha' way back in 2010, when I was first toying around with nautical themes and British Columbian history.

Finally, a gigantic thank you to Zoe Pigott, Linus Pigott, and Shawn Pigott for always being so supportive. Much love to you all!

Manufactured by Amazon.ca
Acheson, AB